“I promise to be on

is here.”

That’s what he’d told his friend Tripp, but if she stepped outta line, all bets were off.

He opened the door when the door to the luxury SUV currently parked on his property opened, and a long, thick and curvy leg appeared, covered in the sexiest pair of thigh-high stiletto leather boots he’d ever seen.

His eyes had just reached her full bosom that her fitted V-neck T-shirt accentuated when she spoke.

“Hi, I’m Keely Tucker. I’m looking for Jacob Chatman.”

Her voice was a rich contralto, smooth and earthy like a fine cognac, and the sound of it wrapped around his name stirred urges he hadn’t much paid attention to while trying to dominate the global horse-breeding market.

“Are you him?”

He opened his eyes and instantly regretted it when wide, whiskey-brown eyes met his. Her body was damn near perfect with curves on top of thick curves. But her eyes, they drew him in like some sort of conjure woman stirring her cauldron, blending magic that would break down even the strongest man to do her bidding.

He shook his head. He’d be damned if he’d forget that women and work don’t mix.

* * *

Designs on a Rancher by LaQuette is part of the Texas Cattleman’s Club: The Wedding series.

Dear Reader,

Brooklyn is headed back to Royal, Texas, for another installment of the Texas Cattleman's Club in *Designs on a Rancher.*

Brooklyn designer Keely Tucker and Royal's very own rancher Jacob Chatman may come from different worlds, but when it comes to their respective professions, they're both the same. Everything is work and work is everything until the two cross paths and begin to realize that maybe making space for the fire-hot passion burning between them isn't such a bad idea after all. Especially when it's just a temporary treat. Keely will be on a plane headed back to Brooklyn in three weeks. What harm could come from them working during the day and spending their nights scorching the sheets?

But when both Keely and Jacob begin to realize that saying "It's all fun and games until someone gets hurt" applies to situationships too, neither is prepared for the consequences of their actions or the blazing desire they can't seem to resist or control. Will they let their good thing slip away or will they both realize that the fire between them is worth risking it all for?

Keep it sexy!

LaQuette

LAQUETTE

DESIGNS ON A RANCHER

Special thanks and acknowledgment are given to LaQuette for her contribution to the Texas Cattleman's Club: The Wedding miniseries.

Recycling programs for this product may not exist in your area.

ISBN-13: 978-1-335-58168-6

Designs on a Rancher

For questions and comments about the quality of this book, please contact us at CustomerService@Harlequin.com.

Harlequin Enterprises ULC
22 Adelaide St. West, 41st Floor
Toronto, Ontario M5H 4E3, Canada
www.Harlequin.com

Printed in U.S.A.

A 2021 Vivian Award finalist and DEIA activist in the romance industry, **LaQuette** writes sexy, stylish and sensational romance. She crafts dramatic, emotionally epic tales that are deeply pigmented by reality's paintbrush.

This Brooklyn native writes unapologetically bold, character-driven stories. Her novels feature diverse ensemble casts who are confident in their right to appear on the page.

Contact: dot.cards/laquette

Books by LaQuette

Harlequin Desire

A Very Intimate Takeover
Backstage Benefits
One Night Expectations
Designs on a Rancher

Visit the Author Profile page
at Harlequin.com for more titles.

You can also find LaQuette on Facebook,
along with other Harlequin Desire authors,
at Facebook.com/HarlequinDesireAuthors!

To all my ladies who are bosses.
This is a reminder that you can
and deserve to have it all.

One

"Finally."

Keely Tucker fell backward onto the plush king-size bed in the middle of her lavish hotel room. After spending the last couple of hours at the Texas Cattleman's Club schmoozing local vendors during a mixer, all she wanted was the peace and quiet of an empty and blessedly silent room.

She lay there, soaking up the silence, wishing she could spend the next few days doing nothing but loafing while watching Netflix. Sadly, she knew there wasn't a chance in hell she'd actually get to do that.

"With everything you've got to do over the next three weeks, it's cute you think you'll have time for television, Keely."

At thirty-one, Keely was stylist to a handful of solid

B-list celebrities, a career she'd proudly carved out for herself over the last decade. After tireless work, and the good fortune of ending up on Ariana Ramos's radar, she was strategically positioned to transition from simply styling celebrities to creating original clothing designs for A-listers.

"You've come a long way from making dresses for your big sister's Cabbage Patch Kids Cornsilk dolls."

Keely laughed at the thought of her older sister Kyrie's most treasured childhood toy. It was a ridiculously ugly thing, but so popular, kids from the late '80s to the early '90s had to have one.

At that time, the doll was expensive for their parents, who were blue-collar workers living in a low-income housing project, scraping by to make ends meet for their small family. They'd splurged to give her sister that doll and she'd treasured it like it was gold. Unfortunately, after spending twenty-five dollars on one doll, there wasn't a great deal of money left over for all the accessories that Coleco peddled to children.

Necessity being the mother of invention, Keely's young self started drawing dresses she imagined her sister's doll wearing. Their mother, recognizing her little girl's talent, pulled out her sewing machine and showed Keely how to turn those pencil drawings into real-life clothes.

That doll was the best-dressed toy in all of Marcy Projects and Keely's very first client. A crucial step that led her to Ariana's door. Thanks to the actress's fame, and all the hard work Keely had put in over the years, her small design house, Low-Kee Designs, was about to hit the big time with respect to the fashion industry.

As excited as she was about her dream coming true, it also meant her work life was about to become more demanding, as if it wasn't high-pressured enough already.

Success wasn't for the faint of heart or the weary. It mostly boiled down to hard work, dedication and sacrifice. This week she'd sacrificed more sleep and energy than she had to spare as she traveled from one client to the next.

She'd started out in her hometown of Brooklyn, New York, before she'd flown to the West Coast to meet with Ariana. After spending a few days in LA to finalize details on the sketches for Ariana's wedding dress, Keely was taking off from LAX and landing in the small town of Royal, Texas.

Keely sighed, trying to quell the restlessness she felt creeping in from the edges of her mind. City-hopping alone wasn't as glamorous as one might think. Perpetual exhaustion wasn't the only result of putting her job first while she stuck to such a rigorous schedule. Loneliness ran a close second as an occupational hazard.

Traveling in multiple time zones in such a short amount of time meant there was no room in her life for the three Fs: fun, flirting and fornication. Case in point was the lost opportunity to accept a dinner invitation from the handsome man one of her friends had worked so hard to set her up with.

Though loneliness was a constant companion, she had to admit things weren't all bad. As tired as she was from all that travel, a smile bloomed on her lips as she thought of her job. At thirty-one, most people couldn't say they were living their best work life and poised to reach their professional zenith. She was grateful for that, so she wouldn't dare let her exhaustion or her desire to connect with another human being on a personal level keep her from living the absolute dream as a stylist-turned-clothing-designer to the stars.

"If you're gonna make this dream work, you can't lie about all night, Keely." She felt around for the phone she'd had in her hand when she dropped like a spent ton of bricks onto the mattress. Just as her fingers curled around it, the device vibrated in her hand.

"Ariana," Keely greeted her client. "You're gonna live a long time. I was just thinking about you."

"I should hope so since you traveled all the way to Royal to finish my wedding gown." Ariana's reply made the grin on Keely's face spread wider. Although the woman was a bona fide Hollywood star, she was still so down-to-earth she could relate to regular folks like Keely. That quality alone made Keely want to create the dress of Ariana's dreams.

"I literally just walked into my hotel room. I plan to hit the ground running first thing in the morning."

"Did Jay drop you off?" Ariana's question made Keely draw a blank.

"Who's Jay?"

"Jacob Chatman," Ariana replied. "Tripp and Ex's

friend. Tripp said he asked him to take you back to your hotel."

Recollection smacked Keely in the middle of her forehead.

"Oh, I told Tripp not to bother. I'm sure his friend is cool and all, but as a city girl, I'm not all that comfortable jumping into a car with someone I don't know."

"How did you get back to the hotel, then? I know you came with Milan in her car and she left well after you."

"I ordered a Lyft," Keely replied.

"Keely." Ariana's voice had a slight note of chastisement in it that made Keely chuckle. "How is jumping into a Lyft any better than accepting a ride from Tripp's friend?"

Keely let out a small sigh before answering. "Because at least with the Lyft, there's some documentable record of whose car I'm in. It's a Brooklyn thing. We don't trust anyone."

Ariana's full and throaty laughter traveled through the line, making Keely's shoulders shake with amusement too.

"Keely." Ariana's voice dropped a note, making Keely sit up and take notice. "I truly want to thank you for coming all the way out here three months before the wedding. It means a lot to me that you're working so hard to make my dress perfect."

Warmth bloomed inside Keely's chest as Ariana put her kind, everyday girl on display. Even a brash city girl like Keely could appreciate the subtle way

Ariana made everyone around her feel like a long-time friend.

"Girl, don't even worry about it. As much money as you're paying me, I would've come down here as soon as you got the ring if you'd wanted me to."

Keely joined Ariana in a full laugh that nearly brought tears to Keely's eyes. Once she caught her breath, she continued. "For real, though. I'm really appreciative of this opportunity you're giving me, Ariana. You could've chosen Vera Wang, Alexander McQueen or Oscar de la Renta to make this gown."

"True," Ariana replied. "But there was something about your designs that just called to me. Those designers are great. But everyone wears them. Me? I like being different. And your designs are the best kind of different on the market, Keely."

"You're damn skippy they are." While Keely was grateful for the opportunity, she knew her work was stellar and no one could give Ariana the dress she'd created for the woman. All she needed now was to find the perfect final touches for it, and Ariana would be the best-dressed bride of the year.

"If you don't mind, while I have you on the phone, I'd like to go over a few final—"

Keely's sentence was interrupted by her hotel room falling into darkness.

"Keely, you were saying?" When Keely didn't respond, Ariana tried to get her attention again. "Keely, you still there?"

"Yeah, but I've got a problem. The power just went out in my hotel room."

Two

"What exactly do you mean I have to exit the hotel?"

Keely stood in front of the hotel's front desk watching the attendant exude the practiced calm that was probably part of his employee training.

"Ma'am, this blackout has created unsafe conditions and we have to evacuate our guests."

Keely's jaw dropped as she processed what the attendant said. "For how long?"

"Indefinitely, I'm afraid. According to the city, they are trying to pinpoint the problem. It could take days to fix."

"Did you just say *days*?" The gentleman nodded, giving her a small smile filled with a lot of regret.

She could feel panic rising, so she pushed it down, trying her best and barely managing to keep a level head.

"All right. Can you at least refer me to another hotel that has suites available? I need a large space for my work."

Keely could see the unwanted answer in his apologetic blue eyes. "I'm sorry, ma'am. But this is a citywide problem. Half the town is without power, and the few hotels that haven't been affected are booked solid."

Keely gave a stoic nod and turned away from the front desk. Panic was climbing up her spine. Determined to get a grip on the situation, she took a breath and pulled her phone out of her back pocket.

With the press of her finger, Keely was dialing Ariana's phone.

"Keely?"

"Hey, Ariana. Apparently, the blackout isn't specific to the hotel."

"We've heard. Are you okay?"

"Physically, yeah. But I'm gonna have to leave the hotel. There aren't any more rooms available nearby with the space I need to work. I may just have to cancel this trip and try to get back down here next month."

Keely was already trying to rearrange appointments in her head to see where she could possibly make time for a return to Royal. Even though she didn't have her beloved planner with her, she knew there weren't any openings in her schedule.

"Before you leave, let me see what I can do." Ariana's voice held a cautious note of optimism that Keely was afraid to hold on to.

"Get your stuff together and be ready to move when I call you back. I promise, we're gonna figure this thing out."

Jacob Chatman slumped down into his favorite recliner, too tired to do anything more than breathe. After helping his staff with mucking stalls, replenishing water and grain, the daily health check of the boarded horses and getting the two newly acquired American quarter horses checked in and settled, Jacob had little energy for anything other than showering before plopping down in his favorite chair.

Tonight he had even less energy to spare than usual after stopping by the TCC mixer to show his face in support of Ariana and Xavier's upcoming wedding.

Closing his eyes, he'd just leaned into the cushions and was about to press the recline button to put his feet up when he heard the familiar, "Jay, where you at?" from his good friend Tripp Nobel.

The stupidest thing I ever did was give that man an access card to my front gate.

He sighed deeply before calling out to his uninvited visitor. "In here." Tripp had been to the house enough that he knew exactly where "here" was. The sound of the man's heavy boots plodding through the foyer and around the corner until he reached the great room was proof of Tripp's acquaintance with both the house and Jacob himself.

"You look beat. Rough day?"

"No rougher than most." Jacob's answer was filled

with exhaustion laced with a little bit of annoyance that his friend was interrupting his peace. Tripp knew the only thing Jacob coveted more than his ranch was his peace, quiet and solitude after a hard day's work. "You need something?"

Tripp's lopsided grin wasn't unexpected. That was both the blessing and curse of friendship. What most people found abrasive, a good friend understood all that growling was just you. Since Jacob didn't have too many good friends to spare, he partially lifted one corner of his mouth into a pseudo smile for Tripp.

"Damn, man." Tripp's feigned offense filled the room, lifting Jacob's mood. Even though he was tired and wanted to be alone, Tripp always managed to make him feel glad to be in the man's presence. "You could at least offer me a beer. I know your mama taught you better than that."

She had. Both Tripp and Jacob had been raised by women who insisted on a clean house, good manners and thoughtfulness from their sons. If you violated any of those expectations, you risked a wooden spoon upside your head. All these years later, those values were still ingrained in them. But Jacob had to admit, after a hard day's work on the ranch, those last two requirements weren't as instinctive as the first.

He prepared to sit up when Tripp held his hand up. "Like I said, you look beat. I know where to find them."

Jacob nodded, and when his friend was around the corner and out of sight, he yelled, "And make sure you wash your nasty hands before you go in my refrigerator."

Tripp's resulting laugh erupting through the halls and filling the air brought on his own laughter. Both their mothers had spoken those exact words to them as boys running into the house looking for snacks after playing outside all day.

Tripp didn't disappoint, coming back with the expected "Yes, ma'am" they both would've rendered to either of their mothers. The sound of the half bath's exhaust fan followed by the splash of running water further amused Jacob. Leave it to Tripp to bring him a good time even when he didn't want one.

Jacob had expected that fact to change since Tripp fell hard for Dionna Reed. Women needed attention, and as happy as his friend was, Jacob wouldn't blame him one bit for focusing all his energy toward Dionna. Yet the gratitude that filled him as he soaked up Tripp's presence in his house threatened to overwhelm him.

Ranch life could be lonely, especially when you're the owner and overseeing everything is your number one responsibility. Jacob had done well for himself, turning his family's once farm into the premier horse ranch in all of Royal. But the cost was giving up any chance he had at finding the kind of happiness Tripp seemed to have with Dee.

Tripp returned with one longneck in each hand, giving one to Jacob before sliding onto the nearby sofa.

"So, what is it?" Jacob's question lingered in the air as they both took sips of their beer.

"What's what?" Tripp's reply yielded a lifted brow and pursed lips from Jacob.

"You offering to bring me a beer because I'm tired screams you want something. So, what's the ask?"

"I guess I can't get anything past you."

"Never could," Jacob replied. "Now, out with it."

"I know this is a huge favor."

"No," Jacob interrupted, "attending that mixer at your insistence immediately after spending all day doing ranch work was a huge favor. Both you and Ex are lucky I love you."

Tripp conceded to Jacob's statement with a nod.

"Unfortunately," Tripp continued, "I'm out of options and you're the only one who can help."

Jacob shifted in his recliner before leaning over with his forearms braced on his knees as he waited for his friend to drop whatever bomb he was holding.

"You might not know it yet since you left the mixer early, but a blackout is affecting nearly half of Royal. I remembered you installing that fancy emergency generator a few years back, so I figured you'd still have power."

Jacob nodded. "True, but the generator hasn't kicked in yet. There hasn't been any power disruption here."

When Tripp tilted his head slightly, Jacob answered his silent question.

"My ranch runs on a separate transformer than the rest of the town. As long as nothing happens to that transformer, I get power. It's too remote out here for me to rely on the town's equipment. Having my own means I control the maintenance and I'm not reliant on the municipality as much."

"Even better," Tripp replied, his response waving in the air like a giant red flag.

Jacob took a long swig from his beer before he looked at his good friend with suspicion.

"I know you didn't come all the way out here to check on the status of my power. A phone call would've sufficed for that. What you want, Tripp?"

Tripp's shoulders shook as a loud huff of laughter escaped his lips.

"Same old Jay." Tripp's comment triggered an acknowledging smile.

"Cutting through the bullshit keeps me sane. Now out with it. What do you want?"

Tripp drank from his longneck, before placing it on a nearby end table.

"You know the entire town is getting ready for Xavier and Ariana's wedding, right?"

"I'm aware," Jacob replied. His ranch may be remote, but even he caught wind of the scuttlebutt surrounding this local-turned-celebrity event. "Even a hermit like me can't avoid all the noise about it."

"Ex never could do anything small." Tripp laughed. "Including his wedding. Some of the vendors at the TCC mixer you dropped in on are already doing prep for the big event. As best man and bridesmaid, it's fallen to me and Dee to try to sort out arrangements for them."

Jacob noticed the sparkle in Tripp's eye as he spoke of his lady, Dionna Reed. Jacob's acquaintance with the woman was extremely short, but even he could tell just how smitten his friend was with her.

"No," Jacob answered before Tripp could even get the question out. "I've got too much work to put some stranger up on my land."

"Jay," Tripp pleaded, using Jacob's nickname to lay on the extra helping of guilt. "The woman who's designing Ariana's wedding dress is stranded. She needs a lot of room to work..."

Jacob shook his head but Tripp ignored him and kept going. "...and since you have a whole cabin you're not using..."

"Doesn't matter if I'm using it or not. She can't come here. I don't have time to babysit some fancy dressmaker from Hollywood."

"Technically, she's from Brooklyn, New York." Tripp's clarification did nothing to quiet the alarm bells going off in Jacob's head.

"I wouldn't care if she was from Timbuktu, she can't stay here."

Tripp hung his head and for just a moment, Jacob worried that his response might've been too strong. Fortunately, the sight of amusement in Tripp's eyes put him at ease.

"Man, do you know how much you sound like our parents with that 'I wouldn't care if she was from

Timbuktu' line? You gotta stop, brotha. We ain't that old."

Jacob groaned before he stood, carrying his beer bottle over to the fireplace where pictures of his parents greeted him. Bixby and Geraldine Chatman were the epitome of getting to reap the benefits of your hard labor. They'd endured the hard and rigid life of farming to keep him fed, clothed and happy.

When they retired a handful of years ago, turning the then farm over to him completely, he'd started working on his dream of converting the farm into a horse ranch. He'd had no idea then how successful and gratifying his accomplishment would be. He also hadn't contemplated on how lonely his success would be either.

Looking down at his parents, he realized they had each other to weather the storm with. Jacob had to make do on his own.

"Tripp, she can't stay here. I don't need strangers on my land." He spoke those words while still staring at the happy picture of his parents, slightly envious of the joy their union seemed to bring them, something he knew he could never have of his own.

He turned around, planning to restate his position when he saw the familiar hangdog face Tripp was making. Something the man had perfected over the years to tug at Jacob's heartstrings more and more.

"Technically she's not a stranger. She's the woman I tried to get you to give a ride to when you were leaving the mixer."

If Tripp thought mentioning that made things better, he was mistaken.

"The one who disappeared without telling you? Oh, she definitely can't stay here."

"Please, man." Tripp had gone into full-blown begging mode at this point. "You're the only one with enough space for all her dressmaking stuff. Help a brotha out."

Jacob tried his best to scowl at his friend, but watching Tripp mock-beg was too amusing to be mad at.

"How many times has your 'help a brotha out' line gotten me into a world of trouble?"

"Too many times to count," Tripp easily admitted. "What harm could having a beautiful and talented woman stay on your ranch do? She needs a big space to work without anyone bothering her, and since you've sworn off women, I know you won't pay her one bit of attention."

Tripp was right. He didn't have the time nor inclination to pay this woman or any woman the time of day.

"Fine, she can stay on one condition."

Tripp's eyes widened with excitement. Jacob could tell the man would agree to just about anything to get Jacob to do this favor for him. And that was exactly what Jacob was counting on.

"If I agree to this, you gotta agree to let me off the hook for all future mixers. I don't wanna hear nothing about me attending another one. Understood?"

Tripp hesitated for just a minute, then reluctantly nodded in agreement.

“Agreed,” Tripp replied quickly. “I promise, man, you won’t even know she’s here.”

“I’d better not,” Jacob responded. “’Cause if I do, I’m taking it out on your hide.”

Three

"You're certain this dude isn't some sort of axe murderer living up in these dark-ass woods."

Ariana's laughter came through the speakers of Keely's rental loud and clear. "While I'm pretty sure that Jacob owns an axe living out there on a ranch, Ex hasn't mentioned anything about him being homicidal."

Keely groaned, hoping she hadn't made an already untenable situation worse by agreeing to stay with this perfect stranger.

"Okay, so he's not a killer." Keely's relief bled through her body. Even with Ariana and her fiancé vouching for him, the suspicious New Yorker in Keely didn't easily trust anything or anyone.

Not that she thought everyone was out to get her.

She'd gratefully not reached that level of paranoia. She was, however, always on the lookout for a scam. If it didn't smell right, Keely's intuition would know before her nose did.

"And you're sure me staying there isn't going to be an issue?"

Keely glanced at the GPS screen, preparing to take the next turn to lead her to her new digs.

"Ariana, your silence isn't making me feel great."

"According to Xavier, Jacob is a stand-up guy, just used to his solitude. So, as long as you stay out of his way in the cabin, he'll be fine."

Keely tapped her fingers on the steering wheel, trying to quell the uneasy feeling she had about this. Although she'd just jokingly asked about any homicidal tendencies, Keely was confident Ariana wouldn't knowingly endanger her.

With only three months remaining before her big day, there was no way in hell Ariana would be able to get a luxury designer to pick up where Keely left off.

Besides, the woman was a good human being. Keely was pretty sure Ariana wouldn't risk her safety because of how kind she was. Ariana's kindness notwithstanding, there was still some anxiety there that Keely couldn't seem to shake.

Chalking it up to the unexpected upheaval of getting caught in this blackout, she blew out a breath and attempted to calm herself.

Keely was great under pressure. She had to be when dealing with celebrities and their clothing. For instance, she was attending an award ceremony when she went to the bathroom and found Coco Jones nearly in tears because the zipper on her designer dress broke. Without even thinking, Keely pulled out the spool of invisible thread and the emergency sewing kit she always kept on her person and literally stitched the woman into the dress.

Relieved, the young actress and singer had taken Keely's name and number just in case she needed her again. She hadn't, but Keely's sure and confident demeanor had stuck with Coco, and when she was in need of a stylist and designer for the next award season, she called on Keely.

Regardless of the nerves in her belly, she had to keep her eyes focused on the goal. There was too much at risk to let nerves keep her from her prize now.

"All right, girl. My GPS says I'm pulling up in a couple of hundred feet. I'll text you if there's a problem."

Ariana signed off, and Keely ended the call just before pulling up to a large wrought iron gate. Pressing the intercom button before the slight rumble of apprehension in her chest made her execute a quick K-turn to get the hell out of Dodge seemed more difficult than hailing a cab at rush hour during bad weather in Manhattan.

The only thing stopping her from giving up was her pride, and the fact that there was literally no place else to go with this blackout affecting most of the town.

A crisp and notably cool "Hello" came through the speaker, reminding her of what Ariana had just said about her host.

Jacob is a good friend of Xavier's cousin Tripp. According to Xavier, Jacob is a stand-up guy, just used to his solitude. So, as long as you stay out of his way in the cabin, he'll be fine.

"He had better be, Ariana," Keely mumbled under her breath, hoping the speaker wasn't sensitive enough to pick up her muffled words.

"I'm Keely Tucker. Tripp Nobel and Ariana Ramos sent me here. I'm looking for a Jacob Chatman."

There was a pause before the speaker crackled to life again.

"Take the road past the main house until you come to the cabin on the other side of the pool."

The voice was abrupt, instantly making her worry. Dealing with assholes on this trip wasn't the number one thing on her to-do list. She hoped it was just the speaker making him sound cold and robotic and not an actual personality trait.

Keely followed his instructions until she drove past a beautiful two-story home with stucco siding and a terra-cotta rooftop bathed in the soft lighting along the trail of the road. She drove past a large swimming pool and spotted the cabin. After idling in the car for a few moments, she grabbed her Prada bag and groaned as she reached for the door handle.

"Big-girl pants, Keely. Big-girl pants. Gotta put them on and notch that belt tight to keep 'em in place."

The reminder was enough to straighten her shoulders and allow her usual confidence to slide through her veins like a loud reminder that she could and would do this because she was awesome at her job. And nothing, not even a real-life growly cowboy, would make her renege on her promise to deliver Ariana's dream wedding dress.

"Tripp, this woman better be as quiet as a church mouse. I can't deal with any distractions. I've got a six-month-old foal coming in and a mountain of intake work to go along with it. I can't have some citified diva getting in my way or getting on my nerves."

"Jacob, you gotta calm down some." His friend's normally easy demeanor was poking at Jacob's annoyance receptors like a petulant child seeking attention.

"I'll be calm when Ariana's fancy dressmaker leaves my property."

Tripp snickered, cranking up Jacob's annoyance factor even more. "Listen, Jay, the city will probably have this fixed soon. Once the lights come back on, she'll be outta your hair and back into a big hotel suite in downtown Royal. Until then, she'll stay in your cabin and you won't even know she's there."

Jacob watched from the window of the cabin as a set of lights from what looked like a pearl-colored SUV in the darkness slowly cut through the night.

He shook his head. A light-colored car on a dusty ranch was a rookie mistake in these parts, making the car and its owner stand out even in the pitch that shrouded the ranch in the evening.

"Jacob," Tripp interrupted him, pulling his eyes away from the window for a brief moment. "Ariana's already talked to her and she's promised me Keely won't be an issue for you. No distractions, no problems. You have nothing to worry about."

For a moment, the silent hope that his friend was right calmed the disquiet rolling around in his head since he agreed to host this stranger. Jacob had learned long ago that nothing and no one was worth the success of his ranch.

He'd sacrificed the good times of most of his twenties to make the Slick Six Stables something his mother and father would be proud of. Something that would continue to keep them in comfort for the rest of their retirement. He wanted his ranch to keep every generation of Chatmans who followed in wealth and comfort.

He'd already accomplished the first two, but the third and most important goal was to have such a prominent brand name that everyone in the equestrian business would be clamoring after a Slick Six Stables–bred-or-trained horse.

That goal was just within reach, with the possible sale of one of his Thoroughbreds to a renowned Kentucky Derby trainer. This could be the career opportunity he needed to go from local praise to global horse-breeding notoriety. With his dream in reach, this was the worst time for any sort of distractions on his ranch.

"We'll see. She just pulled up." The fact that his voice sounded like crunchy gravel under tires didn't escape Jacob's notice. Still, he couldn't find enough give-a-damn to attempt to smooth out his voice and his mood for his friend.

"Good," Tripp responded. "Just remember what your mama used to tell us, Jay. If you can't be nice, be quiet. Don't mess this up for Ariana. If you do, I will never hear the end of it from Ex."

Jacob groaned. If Ex got at Tripp over this, Tripp would in turn grouse until Jacob was willing to do just about anything to shut him up.

"Fine," Jacob spat, hoping his friend understood just how much of a sacrifice he was making for this favor. "I promise to be on my best behavior while the diva is here. But if she steps outta line or gets in the way, all bets are off, Tripp."

"Thanks, man." Jacob could hear the stupid smile on Tripp's face coming through loud and clear on the phone. "Talk soon. Bye."

Jacob slid his phone in his back pocket and took a breath before heading out to the front porch of the cabin.

He opened the door and stepped one foot over the threshold when the door to the luxury SUV currently parked on his property opened, and a long, thick and curvy leg covered in the sexiest pair of thigh-high stiletto leather boots he'd ever seen appeared.

The boot held his rapt attention until its mate joined it and the door closed loudly. The sound made him draw his eyes up beyond the top of the boots to more curves than any woman had the right to possess.

She was a thick woman. And since Jacob liked them thick, he was having a hard time focusing on anything but the luscious curves she had on display.

His eyes had just reached her full bosom that her fitted V-neck T-shirt accentuated when she spoke.

"Hi, I'm Keely Tucker. I'm looking for Jacob Chatman."

Jacob's eyes instinctively closed at the sound of her voice. It was a rich contralto, smooth and earthy like a fine cognac, and the sound of it wrapped around his name stirred urges he hadn't much paid attention to while trying to dominate the global horse-breeding market.

"Are you him?"

He opened his eyes and instantly regretted it when wide, whiskey-brown eyes met his. Her body was damn near perfect with curves on top of thick curves. But her eyes, they drew him in like some sort of conjure woman stirring her cauldron, blending magic that would break down even the strongest man to do her bidding.

He shook his head. He didn't know what the hell that was that had gotten hold of him. But he'd be damned if he acknowledged it, or had him forget that women and work don't mix.

"Yeah, I'm him."

He knew his words were curt, but her slight flinch made him check his inner-asshole and find the home training his mama had instilled in him.

"I hope I'm not putting you out."

He stepped out onto the porch and down the few steps until he was standing in front of her. That was a big mistake. She was gorgeous from afar. This close up, she was absolutely delectable, making him search his memory for the last time he'd held a woman close under an entirely different set of circumstances.

She looked like heaven wrapped up in the most decadent dessert you could think of, and she smelled like a cross between lemon and mint, and everything in him wanted to lean in closer to get his fill. Especially after working around animals all day. Whatever perfume she was wearing was a welcome refresher.

"Glad to see you made it here safe. These roads can be a little difficult for visitors to navigate."

She smiled then, the gleam of perfectly straight white slicing through the country darkness, warming him in places he had no business being warm right now.

"This terrain is definitely trickier than anything I've ever driven on in New York."

"I'll take rough terrain over rush-hour traffic any day of the week."

"Touché."

When her smile widened and the dimple in her cheek deepened, he locked down the smile that was slowly curving the side of his mouth. Too bad the warmth radiating from him, spreading out from the center of his chest to his limbs, wasn't as easy to control. This was a favor. It shouldn't involve him smiling like a goofy teenager in the front yard.

"Why don't you come inside and let me give you a quick tour." When she looked back over her shoulder, pointing to the cargo area of the SUV, he waved his hand.

"Don't worry about it. I'll have a few of my hands

bring your things in. I'm sure today has been hectic enough without you trying to lug heavy suitcases out of your truck."

She nodded, and he turned, extending a hand to help her up the stairs onto the porch. He wasn't prepared for the sharp zing of electricity that the simple feel of her fingers against his palm caused. And when she crossed the threshold, he shook his head and remembered Tripp telling him the dressmaker wouldn't be any trouble.

As he watched Keely walk in front of him, the fitted material of black leggings hugging what looked like a helluvan ass, he wanted to hog-tie Tripp's lying lips together. Because the way his dick wanted to plump up at the sight of her backside in those leggings and boots, Ms. Keely Tucker was most definitely going to be a problem.

Four

"Wow, this is not what I was expecting when Ariana told me I'd be staying at a cabin."

"And just what *were* you expecting?" Jacob's mellow voice was fire on ice, burning away her frozen layers one scorching degree at a time.

Certainly not you.

There was no way she could've anticipated this stranger with his bulky muscles straining his flannel shirt and faded jeans. She definitely couldn't have foreseen how the rumble of his deep voice would vibrate through the night air into her chest and rattle around inside her. And she knew damn well there was no way she could've prepared herself for how absolutely fine this man was.

His skin was a beautiful shade of brown that lay

somewhere between tan and sun-kissed sand. Smooth with its golden undertones, she would give up her next cup of coffee to touch it—considering the way she loved coffee, that was saying something.

"I thought Ariana was talking about a little log cabin without heating or indoor plumbing. She had me imagining I'd be living on the frontier."

He didn't laugh. Stoic and serious as he had been when he'd opened the door, he just stared at her with those dark brown eyes that were so mesmerizing, she had to focus on the cabin just to keep her cool.

She looked around, not just because she was in awe of the design. It boasted a large open space where an eat-in counter separated the kitchen from the living and dining areas.

The walls were wood panels, stained to the perfect color of tanned oak, making the room both warm and bright. There was a stone fireplace with a flat-screen TV she'd swear was at least eighty-six inches, and the soft gray sofa, armchair and love seat made the room seem cozy and lived-in while still elegant.

She could see the stairs leading to a loft, and just beside them were the front windows that had a perfect view of the stone patio area and the pool that sat between the cabin and what she assumed was the main house.

"This is much nicer than a log cabin in the woods."

"Glad it meets your approval." The sarcasm dripping off his response grated on her nerves.

"It's nice, but far. How do you live in such a remote area? I don't know if being this far away from civilization will pose a problem with the dress design and production."

"Beggars can't be choosers."

She turned her head slightly, narrowing her gaze as she pored over his words. Just who in the hell did he think he was talking to? She might be an indie designer on the come-up, but she didn't take shit from anyone. Not even this fine-ass rich cowboy in his wooded palace.

He locked gazes with her, as if they were in a battle of one-upmanship. He was about to say something, something she was sure would only piss her off and escalate the problem. Even though everything in her Brooklyn soul was telling her to cuss his ass out, she couldn't allow anything to ruin the opportunity she'd worked so hard for.

Resigned to extricating herself from the situation without ruffling any feathers, she took a breath, closed her eyes, counted to five and then opened her eyes again. Feeling more in control, she nodded and gave him as kind of a smile as she could muster.

"I know me staying here has to be a great imposition for you and I'm grateful you'd go out of your way to help me out. But the fact that you've growled at me more than once since I arrived tells me you're a lot more bothered by my staying here than Ariana let on. If it's really that much of an issue, I'll find other accommodations."

"I'd like to see you try."

His wry smile kept her eyes firm on his full lips

even when his smart-ass comment made her want to pop him in the mouth.

"You know what? You're an asshole and this obviously isn't going to work."

He raised a sharp eyebrow as if he couldn't believe she'd spoken to him that way. Keely was a lot of things, but a pushover wasn't one of them. She gave as good as she got.

"Gee, don't hold back on my account."

"Trust me, this *is* me holding back. You don't want to see the real Keely let loose."

There was a flash of something bright and hot in his eyes that confused her. It wasn't anger, even though she was certain she was getting on his last nerve. A fact she was proud of considering he'd stomped all over hers.

"Lady, don't blame this all on me. You don't seem exactly thrilled to be here either."

He pulled off his hat, and for the first time, his jet-black wavy hair was free, adding to his sexy factor. For the record, that was just another thing about him that pissed her off. He had no right being as sexy as he was when he was this much of a pain in the ass.

Get it together, Keely. As much as he gets on your nerves, you need him right now.

"My work is really important to me. Making sure this dress is perfect for Ariana is my priority. If I seem ungrateful, it's only because I'm worried. I'm sorry if what I said about the cabin made you think I was somehow being critical of your home."

She watched his shoulders relax just a little, the

small change letting her know he was stepping back behind the arbitrary line.

"I get it. I'm in the process of trying to close a deal on a few horses that will take my ranch to the next level of success. Distractions and inconveniences have a greater impact when you're working at this tier of entrepreneurship."

She nodded silently, glad to have found some common ground with the grumpy cowboy and too afraid of him rubbing her nerves raw to speak. He must've felt the same because he nodded in return before putting his Stetson back on and grabbing the doorknob.

"The kitchen is fully stocked if you're hungry and the master bath upstairs has towels and toiletries. Go ahead and make yourself at home while me and the boys bring in your supplies. I'll make sure we set everything down in the living room."

He looked back over his shoulder, confirming that his stated plan was agreeable. When she nodded, he opened the door and was gone, leaving her alone with her thoughts and her desire. Because even though he annoyed her like a pebble in her shoe, there was no denying that Jacob Chatman was one fine-ass man. Yes, she'd said that before, but it was a fact that bore repeating.

Five

Keely sipped from her steaming cup of coffee, then looked down at the list of vendors on the screen of her iPad mini. She was trying to figure out how to organize her day, except there was one pesky little thing that kept distracting her.

Jacob Chatman.

He came back with help to unload her car as promised, giving her a front-row view of those big arms and tree-trunk legs of his on display. Those images had stayed with her well beyond the few minutes it took Jacob and his crew to bring her things in the cabin. And even though he'd come and gone like the efficient workman he appeared to be, all night long she replayed the ongoing reel of him lifting and setting down trunks' worth of design supplies.

To try to get her mind on work, she'd set up her mannequin and took Ariana's dress from the garment bag she'd laid across her back seat with the utmost care. Now it hung carefully over her mannequin, which was perfectly designed to mirror Ariana's specific measurements, in the center of this luxurious open-floor cabin.

That was a task that should have taken her little time, but because she was so distracted, she caught hell getting that damn mannequin reassembled.

Keely looked at the rest of the unpacked boxes, promising herself she'd get to them by the end of the day. Right now, she had to make a stop at the Rancher's Daughter, Royal's high-end clothing boutique, to find the perfect bridesmaids' dresses to complement Ariana's.

A tap on the door caught her attention, so she closed the case on her device and walked to the other side of the large room to open the door.

Right there in the flesh was the object of her distraction, Jacob Chatman. Today he wore a plain white T-shirt that stretched across the solid wall of his chest like it was painted on. She closed her eyes, instantly reminding herself that this was so unprofessional.

She was a clothing designer and stylist. It wasn't like she hadn't seen well-built men as a matter of course in her workday. Hell, she'd even had cause to glance at a naked form or two all in the name of her job and she hadn't so much as batted an eyelash.

But standing here with this gorgeous man filling

her doorway, and keeping her eyes up and focused on his face, was proving to be harder than it should have.

"Morning, Jacob." She cleared her throat and forced herself to lock eyes with him. "Did you need something?"

He tipped his hat, bringing a much-needed novelty to the moment that distracted her.

Dammit, he was beautiful, slightly bullheaded if their little spat the night before was any indication, but in the dawn of a new day, that didn't seem to matter.

"I just wanted to check on you, see if you need anything before I go back out to the training arena in the back."

"Back out?" She tossed that phrase around before she lifted a questioning brow. "As in you've been out working already?" She looked at the Apple Watch on her wrist and saw it was just after seven.

"Darlin', this is a ranch. We get up before the cock crows 'round these parts."

Did he have to say cock? She was doing so well at pretending he wasn't affecting her. Before her lecherous mind could make her do something stupid like try to steal a glance at his crotch to see what she could see, she stepped aside, letting him in, and headed for the kitchen.

"Would you like a cup of coffee? I just brewed it."

"No," he said quickly. "I've got to get back. I just realized in trying to get you settled last night, I never gave you my number so you can call if you need something. It's a pretty big ranch and as you pointed out last night, we're far enough away from the town proper that it can make going back and forth difficult."

There was something off about him. The hard edges were still there, but there was some genuine warmth there that she hadn't seen last night.

"Is it dangerous out here?"

Keely was a city girl through and through. Even with all her travels for work, the closest she'd come to seeing the woods was when she visited her parents in Washingtonville once they moved out of the city when they retired.

"No. Not during the day anyway." She spread her hands on the nearby counter as she listened to him. "The horse pastures are much farther out, so if you wanna go exploring about, you'll be fine. At night, though, I wouldn't advise you to go off on your own. It's really easy to get lost out there in the thicket of those woods if you aren't familiar with the terrain."

She nodded, then reached over to grab her iPad mini. She tapped the screen until her messaging app opened and handed it over to him.

"Text yourself and I'll lock your number into my contacts."

He looked at the small device in its folio keyboard case, then brought his gaze back to hers with a tilt of his head.

"You actually type on this thing?"

Keely crossed her arms, prepping for whatever nonsense he was about to sling her way. It was too early to fight with this man. But if he threw the first metaphorical punch, she'd be sure to have a blow of her own waiting.

"Yeah. Why?"

He studied her for a moment, as if he was trying to find the words to express himself. "It's just that everything I've seen about you since you arrived last night seems so bold and noticeable. You're at least five-nine. Even though the truck outside is a rental, something tells me your personal vehicle isn't much smaller. You stepped outta that car with stilettos on, and even though you tried to keep your cool last night, you weren't above getting into it with me five minutes after our hellos. A woman like that…this tiny little device that's barely bigger than some phones, just doesn't seem like you at all."

There was something about the way he said "bold and noticeable" that made a spark of fire blaze in her belly, swelling until she could feel the heat moving quickly through her body. They'd spent a handful of minutes together and he could already read her so well.

Who was this man?

She'd worked all her life putting up a hard shell to keep people from really seeing her. Brooklyn was a beautiful place, but it was also cutthroat. You had to be as big, bad and bold as the next person to garner respect. That rule didn't just apply to the streets either.

Even in her family, she'd had to erect that wall to keep their slick words about her chosen profession from getting to her. Her family wasn't terrible. They loved her. They just wanted something practical and reliable for her.

They wanted her to be financially secure, and to them that meant getting a job with a steady paycheck. They weren't elitist. They didn't think that being a designer was somehow beneath their status as medical professionals. No, they would've been just as thrilled if she'd found a civil service job with steady pay and benefits. Knowing what it felt like to struggle to make ends meet, they simply wanted their girls to be secure.

"Astute observation." She turned away from him, hoping he wouldn't observe the flush she felt burning under her skin. "I'm from Brooklyn, where everything is big and bold by nature. You got a problem with big and bold?"

She'd figured by going on the offensive, she'd get better control of herself, finally find a way to not react to whatever it was that set her on fire when she was in a room with him. As soon as she turned around to face him, she'd realized she was wrong. So very wrong.

"I like big and bold."

There was a smile in his eyes and an indecipherable expression on his face that made it hard to tell if he was joking or… Was he flirting with her?

"I live on a ranch in Texas. Everything is big and bold out here."

It certainly was from where she was standing. Jacob was a hulk of a man. He'd clocked her at five-nine, but she was actually an inch taller. Standing in front of him in her sock-covered feet, she had to look up at him. That wasn't usual for a girl who was almost always the tallest person in the room.

"Is that so?"

She was playing with fire and she knew it. But somehow, even knowing it didn't make her pull away. Keely knew damn well she shouldn't engage in any type of flirting with this man that she hardly knew. Less than twenty-four hours ago he'd been a prickly son of a bitch she'd wanted to throw one of her stiletto boots at. Considering they were $2,000 Dolce & Gabbana boots, he'd worked her nerves pretty good to make her want to risk scuffing one of them.

"It is."

They stood there watching each other, locked in a silent battle attempting to see who had the stronger will.

"If you hadn't noticed, I'm a big girl."

By the way his eyes dropped, scaling the length of her body, letting his gaze caress each one of her curves, yeah, he'd definitely noticed she was a thick sistah. And by the barely there hitch in the corner of his mouth, he liked the fact that she had some meat on her bones.

Okay, Jacob, you like 'em thick.

Just as the thought slid across her brain, her common sense snatched her by her proverbial collar and set her straight.

You are not out here to flirt with this man, no matter how mouthwatering he is standing in the kitchen looking like he wants to make a meal out of you. You're here for work. That's it and that's all.

God, she hated her work ethic. It was always spoiling her fun by making her be responsible when all she wanted to do was press her nose into that man's corded neck and see if he smelled like grass and earth, and any other scents one might find on a ranch.

"Well." She could see the moment her response broke the spell and they were back to just being strangers sharing land. "Even big girls like to feel delicate every now and again." When he quirked his eyebrow in disbelief, she smiled. "I'm constantly on the go. This is lightweight, and fits in almost every handbag I own. It's practical and helps me get the job done."

Sensing the change in her playful mood, he nodded, then quickly handled the exchange of numbers, handing her back her device.

"Well, you seem like you've got your day planned out. I'll leave you to it." He walked to the door, grabbing the knob as he turned toward her. "Before I go, it's Friday. There's always a big meal at the house to celebrate the hard work the hands put in all week. You're welcome to drop by and get a plate you didn't have to cook. Grub's on the table at six."

Before she could respond, he was out the door and she was left in her kitchen wondering how the cowboy she'd met last night was getting under her skin with so little effort.

Determined not to get lost in thoughts of Jacob Chatman, she looked down at her iPad mini and opened her agenda again. She started humming the tune of Rihanna's "Work." *That's what you're here for, Keely. Nothing less, and certainly nothing more.*

Six

Keely found the Rancher's Daughter Boutique in the middle of a quaint street. She'd parked closer to the corner, noticing the street sign that marked Main Street in bold letters.

"Wow, so small towns really do have streets called 'Main Street.' I thought that only happened in Hallmark and Lifetime movies."

Amused, she followed the numbers until she was standing in front of the address she was looking for.

A quick press of the bronzed door lever and a pleasant door chime announced her entry. A gorgeous and visibly pregnant redhead with pale green eyes came from the back, greeting Keely with a wide grin.

"Welcome to the Rancher's Daughter. I'm Morgan. How may I help you?"

A genuine smile bloomed on Keely's lips. Although the young woman was elegantly dressed in a sharp pantsuit in a vibrant green, her welcome was warm and friendly, something Keely didn't always find present in the rag industry.

"Hi, I'm Keely Tucker. We spoke on the phone about material and color swatches for the Noble/Ramos wedding."

Morgan's face lit up and she opened her arms, surprising Keely by embracing her as if they were old friends.

"I'm so happy to meet you in person. My best friend and I have been working for the last two days to get the swatches perfect for you. Come to the back and we can get started."

Keely followed Morgan through a heavy velvet curtain into a large room with smaller dressing rooms lining the back, and a round dressing stool in the middle of the room with a mirrored wall in front of it and a sofa and love seat behind it.

Keely saw movement near the sofa that drew her gaze in that direction. There was a woman sitting there whose frame and posture looked familiar as she was hunched over a book on her lap. Familiar eyes and mahogany-brown skin greeted her when the woman looked up. Before Keely's brain could make her speak, the young woman stood, staring at Keely in disbelief.

"Keely, it *is* you!"

Keely chuckled as she laid eyes on a face she hadn't seen since she was a sophomore in high school.

"Zanai James? What on earth are you doing in Royal, Texas?"

Zanai walked over to Keely, wrapping her arms around her. "I've lived here since my father and I left Brooklyn."

Zanai turned to Morgan, whose entire body jiggled with laughter as she watched the two women reunite. "Morgan, Keely used to live in the same building as my aunt Deja. Since I spent every spare minute at Deja's house, Keely and I were inseparable. When you mentioned her name, I wasn't sure if your Keely and my Keely were one and the same. It appears they are."

"Again, it's a pleasure to meet you, Morgan. I'm so glad you were able to still open considering the blackout."

Morgan shrugged. "I grew up on a ranch. This isn't the first time I've lost power. I have a portable generator for the essentials. Thank goodness for credit card readers you can attach to your phone or tablet. Otherwise, business would really be impacted."

"I'm glad you weren't too terribly affected. I've been dying to see what you came up with ever since we spoke."

"And I am excited to show you," Morgan replied. "Sit down and make yourself at home while I go get the swatches. I'm sure you and Zanai can find something to chat about in the few minutes I'll be gone."

As soon as Morgan turned on her Louboutin heels, Keely and Zanai squealed like the little schoolgirls they used to be.

"I hope you don't mind me showing up at your meeting without warning, but when I realized Morgan's Keely might be *my* Keely, I couldn't stay away."

"Are you kidding me?" Keely's reply seemed to widen Zanai's grin. "I'd be so through with you if I found out you were in the same town as me and you didn't stop by. It's been too long."

They finally made it to the sofa, sitting with both their hands linked as if they were afraid they'd somehow slip away and lose each other again if they let go.

"You always said you were gonna design clothes for celebrities. Look at you living your dream, Keely."

Pride swelled in Keely. Zanai had been there from the very beginning when Keely was sketching in her faithful composition notebook. Watching her friend's eyes light up with sincere joy made her buzz with glee.

"So, what are you up to in a town like Royal, Zanai?" The last time she'd seen Zanai had been at Zanai's aunt Deja's funeral. There'd been no time to catch up then with both their hearts so heavy with sadness. Deja may have been Zanai's biological aunt, but she was loved by so many in Marcy, there was standing room only in the chapel.

"I run a developmental psychology clinic for neurodivergent kids."

Keely couldn't help the smile that bloomed on her face. For someone as compassionate as she'd always known Zanai to be, Keely could see how this was the perfect job for Zanai.

"That sounds like a perfect job for someone as smart and kind as you are."

"It is the perfect job for me. I love my clients, and providing them with quality care is truly fulfilling." Zanai waved a dismissive hand in the air. "Enough about me. Where are you staying in town? If you're still at a place with no power, Jayden and I have plenty of space at our place."

Keely leaned forward a bit. "Jayden? Who's that?"

The contented sigh that slipped from Zanai's mouth made Keely chuckle. Even without Zanai confirming it, Keely had a pretty good idea who this Jayden was or, at least, who he was to Zanai.

"He's the most wonderful man to walk the face of the earth, if you ask me." Zanai shrugged and shared a playful wink with Keely. "But I'm deeply biased, so you can't really go by what I have to say."

From what Keely could tell, Zanai's bias told her all she needed to know about her friend's beau. Zanai had always been a reserved, quiet girl. Seeing her sit here aglow in what had to be love, or at the very least, very strong like, Keely was pretty certain it would take an awesome person to bring that out of Zanai.

"Sorry, but that goofy grin on your face says you and Jayden probably don't need me underfoot. Besides, I'm staying at the guest cabin at the Slick Six Stables."

"The Chatman place?"

By Zanai's question, Keely surmised that whole small-town bit about everyone knowing each other had to be true.

"Yeah, you know the owner? His name is..."

"Jacob Chatman," Zanai offered. "He's a friend of Jayden's. I don't know him very well yet. But he's always been kind, very serious, but kind. If he and Jayden are friends, I'm sure he'll take good care of you while you're staying on his ranch."

At that moment, Morgan reentered the room with what looked like two giant old-school photo albums. She set them down carefully on the coffee table in front of Keely.

"Here are the fabric and color samples." Morgan's voice was brimming with excitement. "Even if we don't have the material or color in stock, I can get it here in a handful of days."

Zanai stood up, grabbing her clutch purse before returning her gaze to Keely.

"I'll get out of your hair and let you two get to work."

Keely shook her head, patting Zanai's vacated seat cushion. "No, you won't. Unless you've got a patient waiting, you are going to sit right here so we can catch up while I sort through all these samples. That way I can work and get all the juicy details about how you and Jayden got together."

Zanai folded her arms, lifting a sculpted brow into the air. "Those terms are agreeable. But only if you tell me about all the celebrity men in Hollywood who are begging for your time."

Keely nodded in reply. Those terms were agreeable because there were no Hollywood stars chasing her. There never had been. Keely had been too focused on work every time she'd traveled to Hollywood. There was never any opening in her schedule where she could cut loose and have a little fun and companionship.

No, all there was, all there ever was, was work. A fact she'd been happy about because it meant she was giving 110 percent to growing her brand. But sitting here in Zanai's obvious glow, Keely wondered for the first time if she were missing out on something more important.

Seven

Jacob wiped the same spot on his kitchen counter for the fifth time. To say he was a bit preoccupied would be an understatement.

All throughout supper, even while his ranch hands were being their usually boisterous selves as they sat down to dinner, there was only one thought running through his mind.

Where's Keely?

He was well aware that it shouldn't even matter to him where she was or if she ate or not. But it did. So much so, he kept glancing toward the door looking for her.

That didn't sit right with him. He tried to tell himself it was just the home training his mama instilled in him to be concerned for his guest's comfort. But even he knew that was a lie.

He'd gone to the cabin this morning with the intention of just telling her about dinner and giving her his cell number. His plan was to stand on the porch, deliver his intended message and get back to work. Unfortunately, when Keely came to the door dressed in a simple T-shirt that put her ample bosom on display and a pair of skinny jeans that wouldn't quit, when she'd opened the door and silently invited him in, all he could do was follow.

He didn't like that.

Not one bit.

Jacob wasn't a man who was easily enticed by anything or anyone. The only thing that soaked up all of his attention was work.

Chatman Farms had been reasonably successful when he was coming up. His parents worked hard every day and instilled a fierce work ethic in him. If he wasn't working, he was thinking about work, and that single-mindedness had been the thing to spark his innovation and inspiration for turning the moderately successful Chatman Farms into the popular, and therefore lucrative, Slick Six Stables.

According to his exes, Slick Six was all he cared about. The truth was, he couldn't actually dispute those accusations either. He'd dated. He'd tried his best to treat the women he was seeing well. Inevitably, it never worked out that way. He always became the absent-minded boyfriend, forgetting scheduled dates because he was caring for a sick horse or trying to break a new arrival in. Whichever the case, he'd end up alienating his girlfriends because it was obvious to them that his ranch and his work came before anything else.

That was why he was single. That was why he would probably always be single. He could never put a woman first.

But here he was, the perpetual bachelor, standing in his kitchen while scrubbing an already clean countertop, fixated on a woman who was a perfect stranger.

His ability to focus and effectively close everything out that wasn't work-related was the most important reason for his success. But since the moment he watched Keely step one long, thick, gorgeous leg out of her SUV, his focus had been practically nonexistent.

Realizing he would soon clean the paint off the counter, he tossed his sponge aside, braced both his hands on the counter and dropped his head into a helpless lull. This was his contemplative stance. It usually meant he was about to do something stupid that would get him in a world of trouble.

Breathing deeply, one slow breath after the other, he tried to settle the uneasiness that quivered in his stomach. Just once he hoped that tempting voice in the back of his head that whispered *Do it*, over and over again, would get lost in the soothing sounds of air filling and then leaving his lungs.

He shook his head when the voice became louder than his breathing, knowing full well today wasn't going to be the day that sanity won out over his uncharacteristic impulsivity. Resigned to his fate, he walked over to the sink, washed his hands, then opened the refrigerator door. As soon as his gaze landed on the plate he'd fixed for Keely when he was putting away the leftovers, he groaned.

I'm just being polite. It's only my mama's home training, nothing more.

As he reached for the plate, he could hear the little devil on his shoulder produce a huge, raucous laugh that came deep from its imaginary belly.

You keep telling yourself that, it taunted as it slapped its knee and gave in to another round of laughter. It seemed even his conscience wouldn't let him hold on to his delusions to placate his discomfort.

"Screw it," he whispered before grabbing the plate and marching his way across the expanse of the patio and finding himself standing on the cabin's porch.

Yes, he found himself there. He would never admit to himself or anyone else that he'd willingly go to Keely of his own accord. It was a small fiction that was currently the only thing helping him hold on to his sanity. Because to admit to himself that he was here simply because he wanted to see her again was too dangerous a thought for him to give in to.

Keely stood at the fridge kicking herself for not stopping for something to eat while she was in town. She'd spent most of the day with Zanai and Morgan going through material samples and color swatches, comparing them against sketches of the finalized dress while she and Zanai entertained Morgan with their stories of running around in Brooklyn as kids.

By the time she'd packed up her sketchbooks and a handful of swatches to send to Ariana, she'd completely forgotten about food and headed straight for the Slick Six Stables.

The loud grumbling in her stomach was an obvious protest to that unwise decision. Looking in the fridge and its freezer compartment, she groaned. Everything required prep, and between travel, the mixer and getting herself situated during this blackout, she still hadn't recovered.

She scoured the cabinets until she found unopened jars of peanut butter and jelly and a box of saltine crackers.

"You've had worse in a pinch, Keely. This'll definitely do."

She set her fixings on the kitchen counter when a tap at her front door caught her attention. Even from the kitchen, she could tell who was on the other side of the door by the quick set of taps against the wood and the large yet distinct shadow blocking out the porch lights.

She pushed the curtain aside to glimpse the one and only Jacob Chatman at her door. She might be in a small town where everyone knew each other, but her inner Brooklynite had a healthy dose of suspicion no matter where she traveled to.

He gave a quick nod that made her bite down on the inside of her lip to keep the aching groan building in the back of her throat from leaping out of her mouth. How a nod could be categorized as sexy, she didn't know. Yet everything about it was steady and sure, two things her wayward mind imagined Jacob had in spades when it came to matters of intimacy.

"Sorry to bug you. Just wanted to drop off a dinner plate to you."

He held what looked like a mountain of food beneath aluminum foil.

"Thanks, I really appreciate this."

She stepped aside and he walked into the cabin, following her as she turned around and headed for the kitchen.

She'd hoped the few seconds it took to get from the door to the kitchen counter would be enough to compose herself. Color her surprised when it didn't. In fact, the brief loss of eye contact seemed to make his powerful gaze that much more intense.

"Fixing a snack?"

She shook her head, lifting her gaze slowly from her makeshift dinner on the counter to the sultry half grin sitting on his smug face.

"No, more like working too hard and forgetting the dinner invitation your generous host offered you this morning."

She expected to see him gloating. She certainly deserved it after flaking on his invite. But there, in the depths of his eyes, arrogance was absent. Something akin to…familiarity stared back at her, warming her through and through.

"I thought I was the only person who works so hard, he forgets to eat."

"I've missed so many meals getting caught up in work that if being plus-size was solely about eating too much as society believes, I'd be thinner than this saltine cracker right here."

He didn't say anything. Instead, he silently took her in, all of her. She could feel his hungry gaze slide slowly, oh so slowly, down every bit of her five feet ten inches. Its steadiness made small sparks of desire flutter in the bottom of her empty belly, making her feel just the tiniest bit woozy. Either that, or she was hungrier than she realized.

"Society usually doesn't know what it's talking about." He stretched one of his hands flat against the counter and leaned in. "Plus-size is what we call healthy 'round these parts. Frankly, I don't trust anyone who can willingly walk away from a good rack of ribs, a juicy burger or my mama's banana pudding."

She snatched up another cracker and crunched loudly on it. "I'd kill for ribs right now. And when you say banana pudding, are you talking about like a bread pudding or that banana-flavored Jell-O mess?"

"Alternating layers of sliced bananas and Nilla wafers covered in a milk, egg and sugar mixture and baked to perfection."

"Please stop," she moaned. "Unless your mama is on her way in here with a slice for me, don't torture me like this."

The deep rich tones of his chuckle washed over her, making goose bumps pebble up on her arms. How his laugh managed to be as sexy as the rest of him, she didn't know. But it damn sure was. Even her work-obsessed self wasn't immune to it.

"If she wasn't cruising around the Caribbean with

my dad, I'm sure that could be arranged. But I've got the next best thing."

He lifted the foil cover from the plate he'd placed on the counter.

"So, you can just magically tell when people are hungry and then bring them plates?" Yes, she was teasing the man, who up until this moment hadn't seemed like he had an amusing bone in his body.

Teasing him was far better than giving in to the uninvited want that seemed to move into her body and mind, squatting and getting comfortable, without consulting her first.

"I have many talents."

Keely was certain he did. Everything about Jacob Chatman, from his easy gait and powerful stance, to his broad shoulders and tight waist, reinforced the idea that this man knew how to handle himself at all times.

"I'm sure you do." She pointed to the plate sitting on her counter. "Apparently answering telepathic calls for food delivery is one of them."

He silently went about setting the foil aside, revealing what looked like the best-tasting baby back ribs, baked macaroni and cheese, and steamed cabbage she would ever taste.

"You ordered takeout?"

He scoffed, glaring at her as if she'd kicked his favorite pair of cowboy boots.

"Don't insult me like that. I made everything on this plate."

She pursed her lips, trying to hide how impressed

she was. Yes, men cooked all the time. But the lovely aromas wafting up from that plate indicated that man could burn, and a man who could burn in the kitchen was a rare treasure to find.

"It looks decent."

She was lying through her teeth. It looked like it came straight from somebody's grandma's table. She wasn't about to tell him that, though. The look of defiance settling over the strong angles of his face was too delicious for Keely to come clean.

"I see I'mma have to show you better than I can tell you." Within seconds, he'd somehow made it around to her side of the island. He was standing so close, too close in fact, that his clean and spicy scent pushed away the appetizing fragrance of the food, filling her senses, triggering that heady feeling of floating. "You go'n and sit down."

There was something about the way his voice commanded her, something so visceral it connected with something deep and unfamiliar inside her. Keely wasn't a person who took well to orders. She wasn't a joiner or follower, didn't feel the need to follow the rules of the group just to get along. But the deep rumble of the hint of bass in his voice triggered something inside her that wanted to just relent without question.

For the briefest moment, her inner Brooklynite fought the idea of being told what to do. But the commanding sound of his voice, paired with the stern look that graced his face, soothed something inside her she couldn't explain.

She nodded, doing as she was told, taking the bar

stool on the opposite side of the island counter as she watched him wash his hands, put the plate in the microwave, then set about retrieving cutlery and a napkin to place in front of her.

Keely sat quietly, almost mesmerized by his seamless movement in the kitchen. Yes, this was his cabin. Yet he moved around it with such ease, as if he spent most of his time here and not at the big house where he lived.

She was about to say as much when he returned with her plate and tipped his chin in her direction, signaling her to eat without speaking so much as a word. And she complied, willingly picking up the cutlery and loading up a healthy forkful. Any notion she had of resisting died when she saw the satisfaction her compliance gave him gleaming in his eyes.

She didn't know why it mattered that her acquiescence pleased him. The small lift of his full lips into a barely noticeable smile was like high praise poured over her. It unnerved her, yes. But she was much more intrigued than put off and that in and of itself should've had her running for shelter. Yet she couldn't find the slightest bit of desire to run, so she did what she instinctively knew they both wanted: she ate.

She hummed as the savory and sweet tastes collided on her tongue. Just for a second, the flavor explosion was enough to shake her free of whatever hold this man had on her as she loaded up another forkful while chewing her current mouthful.

"Damn, I take back every slick thing I was thinking about your cooking abilities." She managed to speak around her packed jaw. "This is amazing."

"I know it is." He stood in front of her with his arms crossed and his eyes locked on her. "I told you my culinary skills were unmatched."

She was enjoying the food too much to worry about taking him down a peg or five. He was arrogant, but as good as the food was, he damn sure had a reason to be.

"Did you go to culinary school or something?"

With an arched brow, he cocked his head to the side as he continued to watch her eat. "Yeah. Bixby and Geraldine Chatman's soul food culinary arts program."

Keely picked up a juicy rib covered in a sweet and tangy sauce that was going to leave a mess all over her mouth as soon as she bit into it.

"I'm sure there's a joke somewhere in there meant for me to find." She took a generous bite out of the smoky-flavored meat before continuing. "But this food is too good for me to check for your sarcasm right now."

Her response brought an easy chuckle that she found almost as tempting as the delicious food he'd prepared—almost.

"My parents were big on cooking when I was growing up. Since I'm their only child, they doted on me by teaching me. Anything that could be baked or roasted in an oven, my mama taught me how to cook, and if it could be deep-fried or grilled, or covered in a sauce, my daddy had a recipe for it."

"God bless them." She licked some of the sauce from her fingers, not caring how uncouth she appeared. "I really mean that. They deserve to be nominated for sainthood if they taught you to burn like this."

"I'll make sure to tell them you said so when they get back from their cruise."

"Again," she managed between bites, "I'm sure there's some sarcasm in there, but the food is too good for me to care."

He laughed, stepping away from the counter and grabbing a bottle of water out of the fridge and sliding it over to her. He stood in silence for the remainder of her meal, which should've been weird. She should've questioned why it wasn't. But instead of overanalyzing this scenario like she did everything else, she simply went with it, finding his silent company a comfort she hadn't even known she'd wanted.

When she was finished, he cleared her plate and washed up the dishes. "You cook and you wash dishes. Your woman is a very lucky girl."

"If she existed, she'd probably disagree with you as much as any of my exes on that account."

Even though Keely was in a near food coma, she was lucid enough to catch that fleeting wisp of something in his voice that made her think he might not be joking.

"You can't possibly be trying to tell me you don't have women hanging off you."

"I don't have a problem getting women. Keeping them, however...is another matter altogether."

Stunned momentarily silent, she shook her head, preparing to delve deeper into his meaning. But before she could get her brain to work properly, he nodded, said good-night and closed the door quietly behind him, leaving her watching the door as she murmured, "What the hell just happened?"

Eight

"Everything all right, boss?"

Jacob shoveled the last bit of straw into the stall before turning to his foreman, Matt Santiago, standing just outside the now clean stall.

His muscles ached, and his body was covered in sweat, proof that he had done more than laze about thinking about the beautiful woman squatting in his guest cabin.

"Yeah," he muttered. "I'm good. You need something, Matt?"

Matt stood with a mischievous grin on his face, like he knew something Jacob didn't. He'd been Jacob's first hire when he took over the farm from his parents and began converting it to a horse ranch. His tanned brown skin and ink black hair spoke of his

Mexican ancestry, and the gleam in his dark eyes revealed his good-natured playfulness that made him a good working match for Jacob. He was a hard worker, but he had a knack for reminding Jacob not to take himself too seriously when he became too consumed with the ranch.

"You've been breaking your back since sunup. I'm used to seeing you work hard, but even this is a bit much for you. You wanna talk about it?"

Jacob walked out of the stall, putting his shovel away and pulling his work gloves off, shoving them in the back pocket of his denims.

"Nothing to talk about. I just wanted to make sure everything that needed to get done today was taken care of."

"Or—" Matt raised a finger, ignoring Jacob's excuse for working himself to the bone with little more than a few water breaks throughout the day "—your guest in the cabin has you so rattled you can't think straight."

Jacob shook his head. "You know I don't get wrapped up in women, Matt. Keely is a guest and nothing more."

Matt's grin spread wider. Somehow the sight of it seemed to worsen Jacob's mood. That didn't seem to stop his friend and employee, though.

"Keely is it, now?" The playful note in Matt's voice somehow made Jacob feel more seen, generating the weird sensation to duck and cover. "A couple of nights ago, she was Ms. Tucker when you came to get me and the rest of the hands to help unload her truck. Today she's Keely. Seems like you've gotten cozy with her."

"Matt." Jacob purposely used a deeper tone to try to ward his foreman off. But he could tell by the good-natured gleam in Matt's eyes, the man didn't care a whip about Jacob's attempt at being stern. "Speak your piece so I can go shower, eat and go to bed. It's been a long day."

"All I'm saying is, you've been a bit outta sorts today and I think it has to do with the pretty lady in your cabin. Maybe that's a sign you should be taking the time to have a little bit of fun. Lord knows if anyone deserves a good time, it's you."

Jacob huffed. "I appreciate you trying to look out for me, Matt. But I don't have anything to offer a high-maintenance woman like Keely. She's glitz and glam, and I'm dirt and sweat. She would require a whole lot of time and attention I don't have to give."

Jacob turned, making his way outside of the stables, hoping Matt would take the hint and leave the conversation alone. He didn't need anyone reminding him of what his brain had him thinking of all last night.

The few minutes he'd spent watching Keely thoroughly enjoy the food he'd prepared had been a singular joy he hadn't expected to experience. As someone who worked in the fashion world, he'd expected her to be too prissy to eat in front of him, let alone dig into the plate with the reverence and joy that she had.

The look of serene pleasure on her face and the soulful sounds coming from her took his mind from food to the physical in less time than it took to blink an eye. Instantly, he'd gone from enjoying watching her indulge to wondering if she made those same sounds when she was receiving another kind of pleasure. One he was certain he would give anything to be the one giving it to her.

But when Keely mentioned a fictional lucky woman in his life, it was like the harsh spray of a fire hose slapping him in the face, melting away the fantasy building in his mind.

Sure, there had been women in Jacob's life. None of them were lucky, though, not as far as they were concerned. Each one of them had wanted the one thing he couldn't give. Devoted attention.

"Jay." The pointed tone in Matt's voice meant he had every intention of ignoring Jacob's need to be done with their chosen topic. "You need to blow off some steam, my friend. And if the visitor in the guesthouse piques your interest, maybe you should do something about it."

"I'm busy."

"Yeah," Matt continued. "So is she. That might mean she's game for a little fun too. You'll never know if you don't ask her."

Jacob cut his eyes at Matt, making the man raise his hands up and walk slowly back toward the stables.

"Just think about what I said, Jacob. There's no harm in asking."

Jacob stalked away from Matt, heading back toward the main house. He was in need of a shower, a beer, solitude and peace. If he could make those things happen, maybe they would get him out of this funky mood that had dogged him all day long.

He realized those things might be harder to acquire than he imagined when he rounded the corner of the main house and found none other than Keely Tucker sitting on his front porch waiting for him.

He'd laugh if he found the universe's sense of humor the least bit funny. He'd worked himself to exhaustion today trying to erase their short time together last night. He was just tired enough that he thought he might be able to successfully clear his mind when the object of his apparent obsession was sitting on his porch like the big beautiful distraction she was from the very first moment he'd laid eyes on her.

"Whatever it is, it's gonna have to wait until I've had a shower."

She said nothing, simply nodded, then stood. He walked past her, opening the front door, then moved to the side to let her walk in ahead of him. One look at the large swath of honey-brown skin on display in a pair of denim shorts and he was convinced he'd made the worst decision of his life. There was absolutely no good that could come of this woman being in his house…with him…alone.

Nine

The apology she had for him was on the tip of her tongue when he walked up to the porch. She'd intended to come and talk to him, tell him how sorry she was for making things weird by making jokes about the women in his life. She honestly hadn't meant any harm, but that brain-to-mouth connection of hers didn't always work properly. Keely said what was on her mind. Not to be hurtful, but because lying took too much energy. She wasn't built for things like small talk and diplomacy. Shooting straight from the hip was how she operated.

Except for last night.

Last night, she'd done anything but be honest. If she had, she wouldn't have allowed the hyperawareness she seemed to suffer in his presence to make her try to fill the silence with something cute and sarcastic.

It had worked for a bit. But somehow without realizing it, she'd crossed a line. And since finding a place to stay that had both power and the space to accommodate her work wasn't easy, pissing off her host was the last thing she needed to be doing.

Seeking to prevent more damage, when Jacob told her he needed to shower before he spoke to her, she'd nodded and followed him to the front door. Now, instead of being back at the cabin working on Ariana's dress, she was trapped in this man's living room with the knowledge that he was naked and wet in another room.

And there she went again, thinking about things she shouldn't. Keely paced back and forth in front of the fireplace, trying her best not to imagine Jacob's light brown skin covered in sheets of water as he stood underneath the shower spray. Every time her mind would go there, she'd sketch on the iPad mini with her Apple Pencil, and when the thoughts persisted, she'd walk in front of the fireplace again.

"If you keep that up, you're gonna wear a hole in my rug."

She turned toward the sound of his deep voice to find him standing in the doorway clad in a pair of beltless jeans that hung low on his hips with a crisp T-shirt that stretched against every muscle of his torso, putting every sinew of his solid upper body on display.

"Sorry. Pacing helps me think. I do it a lot when

I'm working on a design that I'm trying to get just right."

"Ariana's dress giving you grief?"

"No," she replied quickly. "I'm just trying to figure out the final touches to take the dress from being a wedding dress to Ariana's wedding dress. I'll know it when I see it. Until then, I'll just keep doodling until I figure it out."

He leaned against the doorway, watching her carefully as if he was trying to figure out the answer to a question he hadn't asked.

"As fascinating as all that sounds, I'm sure you didn't come all the way over here to find me and talk about Ariana's dress design. Did you need something?"

She scratched her head before she began, remembering her mother telling her that was always her sign of contrition. Whatever Keely said after that was usually a heartfelt admission of whatever it was she'd done wrong.

As grown as she was now, she somehow hadn't kicked the habit. Something her mother still thought was cute, while Keely despised the habit because she thought it made her look weak. And weakness couldn't be tolerated when you were trying to build your own empire.

"I don't want to take up too much of your time. I just wanted to stop by and say I'm sorry."

He stood to his full height then, his brows pulling into a pointed V. "And what exactly are you sorry for?"

"I was out of line last night joking about the women you date. I truly didn't mean anything by it. But by the way you shut down the conversation, obviously I said something that bothered you."

She waited for him to say something, say anything. The silence seemed louder if possible.

You said your piece, Keely. Time to leave the man to his brooding alone.

She went to walk past him, but stopped dead in her tracks the moment his long fingers came in contact with her forearm.

He looked down, his brown eyes searing into hers, burrowing through to her very core.

"Don't go." When she didn't respond, he squeezed her forearm with those deft fingers of his, ensuring she couldn't move from that spot if she wanted to. "If we're gonna have this conversation, I'm gonna need a beer. Don't let me drink alone."

He probably hadn't meant those words to sound so loaded, so needy. Their intensity rang inside her head, making it hard for her to think straight. If her brain were working right, she would've carried her happy hips through his front door and back to the cabin. But the neediness in his voice, it called to her like sugar to ants, and she was right on his tail, following him to his kitchen.

He pointed to the bar stools aligned against one side of the counter while he stepped toward his chrome fridge.

"You eat yet?"

"No. You?"

"No. Too tired to cook, so I'm gonna make a sandwich from some of the leftover ribs. You're welcome to eat with me."

"I hope you don't think I came over here seeking food."

"I wouldn't mind it if you did. I hate for food to go to waste but I still haven't learned how to cook for one person."

He turned away, pulling plates and seasoning jars from the cabinets and setting them on the counter and then grabbing a sealed food container from the fridge. Once he grabbed the bread, he layered the fixings in an assembly-line fashion and slid a thick sandwich that required both hands for her to eat.

"Thanks for coming all the way over here to apologize. Wasn't necessary, though."

He chose that moment to bite into his sandwich. She wasn't certain if his timing was based on hunger, or a need to silence himself. Either way, she knew there was more to his words than his easygoing lilt relayed.

"Then why did you leave so suddenly when it seemed we were having a friendly conversation?"

He pushed his plate aside and leaned forward. Even with the counter still between them, she could feel so much heat emanating from him, she was tempted to place a cool hand on his face to test his temperature for herself.

"Dating is a bit of a sore subject for me. I don't indulge in it much."

"I don't understand why not." She blurted out the words before she could catch herself. And since she'd already said as much as she had, she figured she might as well continue with her train of thought. "As fine as you are, I know damn well the women in this town must be trying to break through your gates to get to you."

Something bright flashed in his eyes that she couldn't quite identify. Figuring she'd better quit while she was ahead, she took a bite of her sandwich, letting her food stop her mouth, as her mama always said.

"Thank you for the vote of confidence. My fineness notwithstanding, meeting a woman who can put up with my nonexistent work-life balance isn't as easy as it might seem."

"Meaning?"

He raised his brow, silently asking if she was sure she wanted her question answered. When she nodded, he continued.

"I spend most of my day doing something to build this ranch. Relationships take time and attention I don't have to spare. So, if a woman wants more than a good time every now and again, then I'm not the man for her."

"And by a good time every now and again, you mean…?"

"Sex."

No hesitation at all, he just put it all out there. With her thumb on her chin and her pointer finger tapping at the corner of her mouth, she contemplated his response. To be fair, she did ask him, so she shouldn't have been surprised he gave her an answer.

She couldn't help the cheeky smile blooming on

her lips. Finding a man who was blunt about what he wanted, doing away with the "hey, baby, hey" games a lot of men tried to play as a matter of course, Keely found his openness…refreshing, to say the least.

"I hope I didn't offend your delicate sensibilities by speaking out of turn."

Keely's shoulder shook from the hard bark of laughter bubbling up in her chest.

"Bruh, I'm from Brooklyn, Do or Die Bed Stuy to be exact. The worst thing a man can do is try to run game on me. I appreciate when people just tell me what they want instead of beating around the bush."

"I want people to know what to expect with me. Things can go sideways when all parties involved aren't clear on the expectations."

In that moment, more than anything she could remember in recent times, she wanted to know exactly what a woman could expect from that good time with the sexy cowboy standing in front of her. For a moment, she pondered whether or not it was rude to ask the burning question singeing the inside of her brain.

Something changed in his demeanor as she sat there watching him, pondering her next step. The exhaustion dogging him from the moment he'd rounded the corner to the house seemed to drip away. In its wake was an awareness she couldn't quite describe. Whatever he was noticing or looking for, he hadn't shared. But the intensity of his eyes sliding down her face made her skin burn hotter than the Texas sun during a heat wave, pushing her to ask the question lingering in the air.

"What exactly can a woman expect from you?"

He took another bite of his sandwich, taking his time chewing every morsel before grabbing the longneck he'd pulled out of the fridge and taking a long, slow swig from it that put the thick muscles of his neck on display.

"When a woman is in my presence, she can expect to have my total attention. I might not be boyfriend material, but when I do indulge, I make sure the woman I'm spending time with understands how much I appreciate her company. So, anything I can do to show my appreciation, I will."

Keely was always an imaginative, creative person. It was a trait that had served her well in her life. Tonight, however, it was going to land her in a world of trouble she didn't need.

Sitting here in front of Jacob, listening to him talk about showing his appreciation to a woman, her overactive imagination was banging against the mores of her barely there tact, desperately wanting to know what that appreciation looked like in real time.

"You could teach some of the men I've encountered a lesson."

He lifted his brown eyes, encouraging her to elaborate, and even though she knew she shouldn't, she took a swallow of her beer for courage and continued.

"I travel a lot for work. I'm never home more than a couple of weeks at a time. The men I meet that want to treat a woman well also want commitment. My career is just taking off. I can't focus on anything other than work."

"And the men that don't want to treat a woman well?"

She broke away from his dark gaze to peel an edge of the bottle's label away from its cool surface, trying to figure out how to answer him without seeming desperate or uncertain of her own mind.

Keely knew what she wanted. She just hadn't found anyone willing to give it to her yet. Or maybe she had? Jacob chose that moment to walk around to her side of the counter, leaning his hip against the marble and staring down at her with such desire she had to wonder if for once she'd met a kindred spirit that understood her boundaries where relationships were concerned.

"The men who wouldn't mind the friends-with-benefits thing only seem to focus on the benefits and not the friends part. Just because I don't want a ring doesn't mean I want to be treated like I'm disposable either."

He moved his hand slowly toward her face, giving her more than enough time to pull away if she chose. He needn't have worried about that. She wanted to know what Jacob's touch felt like, if only something as innocent as a fingertip caressing her cheek.

Fortunately, she didn't have to concern herself about innocent touches. When his finger and thumb clasped her chin, bringing her gaze up to his, there was no mistaking the fiery need burning in his heated stare.

"There is nothing disposable about a woman as

gorgeous as you. Any man that doesn't recognize that is a fool who doesn't deserve a second of your time."

"For a man that just met me a few days ago, you seem mighty certain of your assessment of my value."

"You saying you disagree with me?"

"Not at all," she replied. "I know my worth. I'm just questioning how you can be so certain of it after spending so little time with me."

He didn't drop his gaze, didn't retreat into some slick pickup line. Instead, he scrutinized her face as if he was committing every line, slope and angle to memory for his assessment.

"Only a fool could stand in your presence and mistake gold for rusty old tin. I would never make that mistake."

By the drop in the timbre of his voice, she knew he was going to kiss her even before he moved slowly but intentionally toward her. By the time his mouth hovered just above hers, she parted her lips in hungry anticipation.

She knew she was too eager, that her best bet would've been to play it cool and reserved as if she didn't care. But damn her need to present a put-together facade, she wanted his mouth on hers and she wanted it now.

Too desperate to know if he tasted as good as he looked, Keely lifted her hand, curling each finger into the cotton of his crisp white T-shirt, dragging him down and pressing her lips to his.

If he was put off by her forwardness, he didn't let on. Instead, it seemed to urge him on as he threaded eager fingers into her loose strands, tugging just tightly enough to keep her exactly where he wanted her.

When she moaned in appreciation, he pressed his lips harder against hers, moving them with a controlled urgency that both satisfied her while making her ache for more.

She spread her fingers wide across the hard plane of his chest. This wasn't sculpted muscle from being a gym rat. She was certain Jacob's solid physique didn't come from staring in a mirror all day while he curled hand weights. She'd bet his solid frame came from roping cows or whatever it was that cowboys did on a ranch all day. Whatever it was, she was grateful for what resulted in a gorgeous specimen of man that was waking up parts of her body she'd apparently neglected for far too long. Because the taste of this man's lips and the rugged smell of spice and soap that wafted up from his skin was an intoxicating mix that made her blood pulse and sex clench.

Girl, you did not come here for this.

True, but she couldn't say she was all that upset at the turn of events either. Not when every nerve in her body was vibrating with desire.

When he gentled the kiss, pulling back slowly, her senses were so overrun she could hardly distinguish light from dark.

She blinked several times, trying to get her vision to clear and her eyes to focus again. Still under the influence of Jacob's kiss, she closed her eyes, leaning into the hard wall of his chest.

"I think you kissed me blind."

She could feel his laughter move through him as he held her closer.

"I'd like to take credit for that." He whispered just loud enough for her to hear. "I haven't enjoyed kissing someone like that in a while. But I think your temporary loss of sight has more to do with a power loss than my kissing technique."

"Wait, what?"

He set her back from him, tracing the side of her jaw. "Seems like the Slick Six is experiencing a blackout too."

Ten

Jacob passed his flashlight beam once more over the backup generator, making certain everything was in working order.

He'd cringed at the exorbitant cost of the thing when he'd had it installed. That was then. Now, he was grateful he'd had the foresight to purchase it.

He looked over to his side to see Keely standing next to him with her arms crossed and worry pinching her brow into a sharp V. For him, being out in this kind of darkness was a usual, comforting thing. He imagined being from the city, where the lights were always bright and plentiful, this kind of night had to be unnerving if not outright alarming.

"Everything working okay?"

Her voice was steady, but he could see the concern in the rapid movement of her dark brown eyes. He reached out his hand, hesitating slightly before placing it carefully on her biceps.

Just before the blackout, he'd had his mouth plastered to hers in the most titillating kiss he'd ever experienced. But Keely's agreeing to kiss him in the confines of his kitchen didn't mean he had the right to touch her anyway he wanted, wherever he wanted, even when his only desire was to comfort her.

"Everything's working as it should. There's only one problem I can see."

"What's that?"

"We have enough propane to keep the lights on until my scheduled propane delivery next week—"

"That doesn't sound like a problem." He smiled, trying to keep from alarming her. Keely was bright, bold and loud, and as much as he hated those qualities on most people, they were downright attractive on her. So, seeing her with the slightest bit of concern dampening her natural boisterous persona didn't sit right with him.

"You didn't let me finish. We can keep the lights on until my delivery next week if we shut down power in the guest cabin. Running electricity in both residences is gonna consume a hell of a lot of gas in a short amount of time."

"Are you evicting me?"

"From the guesthouse? Yes. From the ranch? No. You'll just have to stay in the main house with me."

"Ugh," she groaned. "Why does the universe hate me?"

He chuckled a bit. Her dramatic display of frustration was entertaining if nothing else.

"I'm sorry the idea of staying in my guest room is so unappealing."

She shook her head. "It's not you." Her voice was soft and resigned, as if she'd just decided fighting wasn't worth the energy. "I'm very grateful for your hospitality. The issue is space. Space and solitude."

She must've noted the confusion in his furrowed brow and narrowed gaze because she continued without being prompted.

"Ariana's dress is huge and white, and needs to be guarded like a national treasure. She's a celebrity. The tabloids would do anything to get a sneak peek at it before the big day. I can't let that happen. Moving to another location, especially a house where other people have access to it, will increase the chances of the dress getting leaked."

"Is that all?"

She looked a bit annoyed if the sharp glare she aimed at him was any indication. He held up his hands quickly to slow the fire he could see growing in her stare.

"My great room is large enough for you to work, and the double doors have a lock and I'm the only one with a key. You can keep the room locked up to keep the gown safe. I also have blackout blinds on the windows, so we can make sure no one can get a sneak peek of the gown before the wedding day. Does that work for you?"

She blinked at him, as if she were still attempting to process everything he was saying.

"Yeah, that works. Thank you."

"You sound surprised I'd try to help."

Her face was open and bright, and even without the beam of the flashlight, he was certain he'd still be able to make out every glorious angle of her beautiful face.

"To be frank," she began.

"Do you know any other way to be?" he asked, hoping she didn't find his sarcasm offensive.

When she chuckled softly, warmth spread through him. "Actually, I don't. Being forthright is a personality quirk of mine."

The smile on her face lightened his mood even more and he had to wonder if he should be so concerned that a mere smile from this woman could make him feel light and free.

"I'm not surprised you'd try to help me. You seem to be someone who looks out for people. That first night I was here when you and your hands came to unload my truck, you were very kind and open with them. That kind of connection isn't always present between employees and bosses. I'm just surprised you didn't look for another option that would get me off your ranch and out of your hair."

She was right. He could've called around to see if

he could find somewhere else for her to stay. But the truth was, the thought had never crossed his mind. He'd never once thought of her being anywhere else but with him.

He should be unnerved by that. But he wasn't, and he wasn't naive enough to ignore why. The kiss they'd shared, along with the conversation where she'd told him she didn't want to be treated as disposable, had flipped some kind of switch in him. Suddenly, he wanted her around if only to prove to her that he would never be the kind of man to treat her so poorly.

He wouldn't tell her that, though. He knew from experience that telling a woman something like that gave her ideas he couldn't possibly entertain because he wasn't boyfriend material. He wouldn't play games with Keely like that. Even though he'd only known her a short time, he had a great deal of respect for her. So instead of telling her the truth and risking her misunderstanding his meaning, he simply said, "I'm not that much of an asshole, Keely, that I'd turn you away in your time of need. Especially when I'll be out of the house most of the day so the only time our paths will cross will probably be at dinner. I think I can put up with that little intrusion on my solitude for however long you're here. How about you?"

She smiled again, nodding her agreement. And as they made their way back to the main house, he prayed his assessment was right. Because Keely was temptation on legs, and he had too much to lose by giving in to his baser desires.

* * *

"Is that the last box, Matt?"

"Yes, boss." His foreman came over to help Jacob pack up all of Keely's things and get them settled into the great room. "You need me for anything else?"

"No, Matt. Thanks for coming out this early and helping me out."

"You know I always got your back, boss."

Matt may have called Jacob *boss*, but they both knew the man was more than just an employee. He was a treasured friend, which was probably the only reason he got away with half the things he said to Jacob.

"'Preciate, man. Since you came out here so early, take the morning off." Before Matt could resist, Jacob held his hand up. "I'll take care of your duties."

Matt tipped his head toward Jacob with a jubilant smile plastered across his lips.

"Shoot, you don't have to tell me twice. I'll see you this afternoon."

Matt clapped him on the shoulder just as Keely made her way into the kitchen.

"Thanks for all your help, Matt." Jacob turned to see the gracious smile on her face and the relaxed features that made Keely appear more comfortable in his ranch home than one would think a city socialite like her would be.

"Welcome, Ms. Keely. I'm just glad you won't be alone in all that darkness. Holler if you need anything else. Jacob knows how to find me."

She nodded and waved as Matt made his exit, sharing the kind smile she'd just gifted Matt with Jacob.

"He's such a nice guy." Keely's comment brought a wry smile to Jacob's face.

"That's because you don't know him well enough. He's a great worker and a better friend, but a royal pain in my ass all the same."

"Good friends often are." She looked around the kitchen before bringing her gaze back to his. "I really appreciate all the trouble you've gone through to accommodate me."

"Wanna make it up to me?" Her pointed stare made him shake his head. "Don't worry. It's not that kind of proposition. Since we've gotten your things sorted in the great room, how about going on a ride with me?"

The suspicion on her face went from paranoid to cautious as she contemplated his request. He'd met a few New Yorkers in his travels and their suspicious nature of anything friendly was a great source of entertainment for him.

Keely wasn't off-putting. In fact, her open smile and boisterous nature drew you in like a carefully placed lasso on a calf, tugging at you until you couldn't help but surrender to her call. But even though everything about her pulled at you, you could tell by the cut of her eye and the intensity of her stare that she was always attempting to anticipate your next move.

"I'm taking over Matt's morning duties since he came over and helped me get your stuff moved over here. I need to check the perimeters of the land, make sure the posts are secured and safe so none of the horses we let roam free in some of the open areas get injured. I figured after all the work you put in setting up the great room, you might've wanted to take a break and take a nice horseback ride with me."

She folded her arms, tipping her head back and forth before she raised her gaze to his.

"That depends."

"On what?"

"On whether you've got a really even-tempered horse that won't throw me. I haven't ridden since I was a kid."

Horseback riding was usually something people in elite circles indulged in frequently. He was slightly taken aback to hear she hadn't ridden in so much time.

"I do." His reply seemed to calm something in her and he realized this wasn't a show. She really was concerned with the temperament of the horse. "Her name is Tildy and she's the sweetest horse you'll ever find. She loves people, and if you feed her a treat, she'll be loyal for life."

Besides his mother, Tildy was the most loyal female he knew. Because she was so sweet, Jacob was extremely protective of whom he paired her with. If a rider was too hard or vigorous, they didn't get to ride his sweet Tildy. But somehow, he knew that Keely would appreciate the old girl and be as kind to her as Jacob was.

Keely was a person who paid attention to detail. He was sure that skill had to be useful in her line of work. She noticed enough about him to understand that something was wrong and she cared enough to seek him out to smooth things over. He didn't know why, but her actions had meant something to him.

Now, he wanted to spend a little more time in her presence.

He ignored the warning bells that were clanging loudly in his head, trying to remind him that he didn't have time for whatever it was he thought he was doing. Then he watched a smile bloom slowly on her face, the single gesture making warmth and contentment spread through his chest, and he knew right at that moment there wasn't an alarm bell loud enough to make him withdraw his invitation.

"Sure." Her easy response lured him even more into the depths of the fog he found himself in when he was near her. That fog was thick, surrounding him, blocking out anything else from his senses but her. "I'll ride with you. Let me just run upstairs and change into something appropriate."

Appropriate.

As she turned around, heading up the back stairs to the guest room, all he could think of was that the titillating thoughts running through his head as he watched her perfectly rounded ass climb the stairs were anything but appropriate.

Eleven

"Damn, this place is big."

Keely stepped inside the stables, turning in a circle as she took in the wide space. Not that she had much to compare it with. She'd only ever ridden when she'd gone on her high school's annual field trip to a small farm upstate. The rickety old building where the handful of horses on that farm resided wasn't even in the same category as this large horse palace that boasted of high ceilings, a loft that bordered the entire interior structure, and stalls lining a long wall.

"It's a'ight." His knowing smile belied his faux humility. He knew damn well this place was amazing.

"How many horses do you have here?"

"In here? Five." His response made her take another glance around the interior. This place was too big for five horses.

"We have three stables on the property. This one houses ten. It's the smallest. My personal stock is kept here. The other two are for sales and boarders, respectively. They can house up to fifty horses each."

Keely's mouth dropped open. Again, she had no context for how many horses could or should be on a ranch. But she certainly didn't think having more than one hundred horses on your property was to be expected.

"Do you really have enough room for that many horses? I'm not talking about the stalls. I mean, I imagine they need space to run around or something."

He nodded casually as he led her down the hall. She took in each stall whether it was occupied or not. From growing up in Brooklyn, to all the traveling she did now as a stylist and designer, her travels had never taken her to a bona fide ranch. The rural landscape and lifestyle were more foreign to her than any country she'd set foot in beyond the borders of the United States.

"They do. A safe measure is ten horses per acre. At fifteen thousand acres, we can technically house fifteen hundred horses."

She turned to him, ready to interrupt, when she saw his mouth curl into an amused grin.

"No, we never take on that many horses at a time. We may have the acreage to support that many, but not the staff. I employ about sixty full-time hands. A third of them live on property and the rest commute in every day."

He walked ahead of her as they neared the middle of the stables, grabbing an apple from a nearby table.

"Tildy girl, I've brought you some company."

Keely watched a golden beige pointed head with a white snout peek out of the middle stall on their right.

"Tildy girl, you ready for a visit?"

Jacob got close enough to rub the animal's snout. Apparently, she enjoyed Jacob's petting her because she pushed her head in his hand, encouraging him to stroke her again.

Lucky girl. Keely shook her head at her ridiculousness. *Gosh, Keely. You know things have been running slow in the man department if you're jealous of the attention he's paying a horse.*

Once she stopped lamenting the fact that the horse was getting more action than she was, Keely took notice of the gentle timbre of Jacob's voice as he greeted Tildy.

Here was this big man, standing well over six feet with a wide and muscular body to boot, and he was speaking in hushed tones to this great animal who was soaking up all his affection and sharing a bit of her own. She kept bobbing her neck and almost nuzzling the side of Jacob's face.

"That's my good girl. I'm happy to see you too." He waved Keely toward him, pulling her close to him, but standing between her and the stall. She realized he was trying to make her feel safe around Tildy.

That kindness made her want to settle against his side. But since she was trying to keep things platonic, she stayed where he'd positioned her.

"Do you want to get closer to Tildy so you can meet her proper?" When she nodded, he held out his hand and pulled her close enough that their shoulders touched. A brief sizzle of electricity sparked between them and Keely had to use all of her willpower to not jump away in surprise.

"Always approach a horse from an angle. You want to make sure they see you and know you're coming. Tildy weighs about a thousand pounds. You don't want something with that kind of heft surprised by your presence."

Again, she nodded, paying close attention to his impromptu lesson on getting comfortable with horses. She was certain going riding when she was younger was born out of the invincibility teenagers believe they possess. But as a grown woman who understood a healthy dose of fear could save your life, she was grateful for Jacob's care.

"Tildy is a Norwegian fjord horse. This breed is short, no more than thirteen or fourteen hands, but built stocky. It can carry a full-grown adult and then some. These horses are also bred for their calm temperament. They don't spook easy, making them good for first-time or novice riders who need to get used to being up close and personal with our big, four-legged friends like my girl here. When you're ready, give me your hand and I'll help you pet her."

He reached out to her, slowly curling his fingers around hers until her entire hand was swallowed in his. He gave her hand a gentle squeeze before laying it flat on the horse's shoulder.

"You wanna make sure you pet her in the direction of the grain of her hair. Doing otherwise can be uncomfortable for her. So, start at the top of her neck and brush down toward her shoulder. Make sure your strokes are slow and soft."

She listened to him; his deep voice was so soothing. She couldn't blame the horse from being lulled into ease. Keely's own nerves calmed to the relaxing tone of Jacob's voice.

He continued to talk her through more steps to getting acquainted with Tildy, including feeding her apple slices from a flat gloved hand and attaching a lead rope and pulling the golden-haired horse from her stall to the tack area at the back of the stable. By the time he'd put Tildy's tack on, Keely felt relatively comfortable, and the way the kind creature began to seek affection from Keely, budging her hand the same way she'd seen Tildy budge Jacob's, Keely felt she'd probably just made a new friend.

Jacob saddled up his horse, a large black beauty he'd called Midnight, and they walked them both outside in the fresh open space. After demonstrating how to mount a horse, and giving her pointers on how to make the ordeal less awkward for herself and Tildy, she was soon sitting astride Tildy. After instructing her on how to hold the reins and how to get Tildy to move, Jacob mounted Midnight.

"Since you're learning, we're not really gonna ride today. We'll just walk around at a gentle pace."

Her nerves started to flare and he must have somehow recognized her apprehension because he reached across to her, silently asking for her to place her hand in his. When they touched, and she felt his warmth and confidence flowing through her, their gazes met.

"I'm a man of my word, Keely. You can trust me when I say I won't let anything happen to you. You're safe with me and Tildy."

For no other reason than he'd said it, Keely believed him. If she were thinking clearly, she'd acknowledge how out of character for her that was. But Jacob's firm yet soft hold on her hand made her forget about all the reasons she shouldn't blindly trust this man. Namely, because anyone who said "trust me" generally couldn't be trusted farther than they could be thrown.

"So, is there anything in particular we came out here for, or did you just really want to give me an impromptu riding lesson?"

Jacob glanced at Keely from the side, finding himself fighting the smile her blunt words brought to his lips. He was beginning to notice this lightness in his chest whenever he was around her. It was persistent, scraping away at the loneliness that had settled there.

He'd always believed his penchant for solitude was a blessing. It kept him focused on his work, and focusing on his work had helped him build this ranch from nothing. The Slick Six had become everything to him. But listening to and watching the easy yet daring way she approached everything, it was hard for him not to acknowledge her presence offered him something good, something that had been missing in his life for so many years, he hadn't realized how vital it was until this moment: companionship.

"We're going to check on the transformer. The ranch isn't connected to the city's transformers."

She turned her head to him while looking upward as if the sky was gonna give her the question she was searching for. When her soft brown eyes connected with his, he realized she wasn't searching for the question. She knew exactly what she wanted to ask. She was trying to decide *how* to ask the question.

"Keely, you don't have to censor yourself. If you wanna ask something, ask it."

Her shoulders relaxed a bit, telling him his assumption had been correct.

"I get being a diligent landowner and checking in on your property. But don't you think checking on a transformer is something a professional should do?" She lifted a sleek brow, drawing his attention to it, causing him to fight the urge to stop and reach out to touch it.

He cleared his throat before speaking, trying his best to hide the impact her voice and forwardness had on him from her, but himself too.

"Yes and no."

She nodded, beckoning him to continue. Usually his one- or two-word answers would've been as far as he would've bothered going by way of an explanation. But again, this was Keely, and he was finding her harder and harder to resist.

"This is something a professional should handle, and if the problem is too complicated, I'll definitely have to wait for someone to come out here and check on it. But with the town's power still out, electricians are in high demand right now. This way, if it's something minor, I can get it fixed now."

"Ready to be rid of me already?"

He didn't answer immediately. He needed time to process the answer. If she'd asked him this when she'd arrived a few days ago, the answer would've been a resounding yes. But after knowing what her luscious mouth felt like pressed against his, having her around him wasn't such a difficult task.

"If I wanted you gone, Keely, you would be."

Her face was impassive, and he wished he knew her well enough to be fluent in her particular code.

Before he could explore that thought further, the outpost cottage came into view. She followed him, watching him dismount, and when he was standing next to her with his arms stretched out, she surprised him by repeating the same movements herself. Granted, she wasn't as graceful as him, but the fact that she'd been game to try any of this won her all the bonus points in his book.

"Are we visiting someone before we get to the transformer?"

"No," he replied. "This is one of a handful of cottages placed on some of the more remote locations of the ranch. The last thing you wanna do is get stuck out here with no means of communication or provisions. We keep these cottages stocked with nonperishable food and a landline just in case someone needs help, or when one of the hands has to work out here."

She opened her mouth to ask another question and he lifted a pointed finger to stop her. "And to answer your next question, the transformer is behind the cottage."

He grabbed the saddlebags from both horses, resting them both on the verdant grass before he took their lead ropes, petting both of them as he spoke in the same hushed tone he had in the stables.

"Now, I'm depending on you two to behave while me and Ms. Keely go check on a few things. Can you do that for me?"

Midnight tapped one of his front hooves and Tildy bobbed her neck, pushing into his hand as he gave her a good rub.

"All right, now. Remember to come when I call." He removed their lead ropes before giving each of them another comforting pat. "Go play, y'all."

She watched the horses gallop away, then turned her bemused gaze back to him.

"Do they really understand what you're saying?"

"I've had them both since they were foals. Trained them myself. They understand the commands they're given. But more than that, they understand my body language. If I'm petting them and talking gently, they don't sense any fear or danger. Horses are very in tune to the emotions of humans."

They made their way inside the one-room cottage. Unlike the cabin behind the main house, Jacob had had these cottages built for utility instead of luxury.

There was a small sofa and two recliners in the center of the room, each flanked by end tables. A modest TV hung over the fireplace, completing the living area. The kitchen was a corner in the east side of the structure. It housed a small kitchenette table with four chairs, a small gas stove, a refrigerator and a chopping block that couldn't have been more than three feet long.

Behind the couch there was a double bed against the wall with a nightstand on each side of it. He tried really hard to ignore that particular piece of furniture. With Keely standing in this room, it was far too tempting. He was here to do a job, not engage in some sleazy seduction fantasy.

"Here's the place." He waved a hand around the entire expanse, stopping briefly to point to a door next to the bed. "That's the washroom, if you need it. Since the power is out, I wouldn't trust anything in the fridge. I've got a few provisions in the saddlebags if you get hungry, or I could pull out a can of something from the cupboard."

She crossed her arms, staring him straight in the eye with that unforgiving confidence of hers. It might've come off as arrogant and condescending on most women. But on her, it was like a shining light that drew you in from the darkness.

"Jacob, I didn't get my happy hips on a damn horse just to keep you company on the ride. I plan to be out there with you."

She leaned into one leg, jutting one of her aforementioned hips out, making his hand itch with the desire to touch it, rest up on it, hold on to it.

"Keely, other than the ones from Hasbro, do you know anything about transformers?"

She pursed her lips into a sexy pout that had Jacob more than a little fixated on their shape and how soft and silky they were.

"I don't know anything about electrical transformers. But I can hand you tools, and if you manage to get yourself electrocuted, I can call for help."

"Fair enough," he relented as a soft chuckle escaped his lips. "Come on with me if it suits."

Amused by her chastisement, he headed toward the back door. As soon as he stepped outside, he knew exactly what the problem was. A few large tree branches from a nearby oak lay on top of and littered around the sides of the metal encasement that protected the transformer at ground level.

When he reached the encasement, he didn't see any physical damage severe enough to interrupt power.

"I don't think anything's broken. But the vibrations from those branches dropping from high up could definitely have loosened or disconnected one of the connectors."

"Can you fix that?" He could hear the slight apprehension in her voice, and everything in him wanted to hold her and soothe it away.

"Yes, I can fix that. Let's just hope that's the issue. Otherwise, we'll have to wait for an electrician to arrive."

They set about working, Keely standing by his side, helping him remove the branches she could and stepping out of his way when he grabbed those that were too heavy for her to lift. He was glad for her help. It had taken a good block of time to get the transformer case cleared of the debris and without her, he might have been out here past dark trying to get this thing up and running.

He finally opened the case, scanning the darkness of the internal chamber with a flashlight. Relief flooded him when he saw two disconnected cables on the transformer.

"Is it worse than you thought?"

The sound of her voice made him look back over his shoulder. She was standing, but leaning hunched over at the waist with her hands on her knees, putting all the golden-brown skin of the top of her cleavage at his eye level.

There wasn't anything remotely erotic about her intentions. This was just her trying to help him get the lights back on at his ranch. But being this close to her was short-circuiting his brain. He was having a time forming words, but his traitorous cock seemed to be working just fine as it strained against his denims.

"It's a…it's…" He wet his lips, trying to get his brain to focus on the transformer and not her. Unfortunately, that was easier said than done because Keely was wearing the hell out of that V-neck T-shirt and he was a grown man who adored and appreciated a beautiful bosom. And from just this little peek, he could tell hers was better than most. Beginning to feel like a creep, he shook his head and focused his eyes on the transformer. "It's exactly what I thought it would be. I just need to tighten these cables and hopefully that'll restore the power."

"Good," she responded. "Because it's hot as hell

and we've been out here all day. If I sweat any more, I'm gonna start smelling like who did it and ran. I need a shower in the worst way."

Great, exactly what he didn't need. Images of Keely naked, covered in suds and water. Was she trying to kill him?

"I'll work as fast as I can. But sunset is approaching soon. We ate up a lot of time on our ride and clearing the debris. Are you okay with staying out here with me, or do you want me to call one of the men and have them come take you back to the house?"

He turned, waiting patiently for her answer. He wasn't exactly propositioning her. But by the spark in her eyes, he could tell she was contemplating the unspoken invitation lining his offer.

The delay between him asking the question and her answering seemed to stretch out for hours, even though he knew in his mind it couldn't have been more than a few seconds. Still, he didn't push. He gave her all the power in this situation because ultimately, he wasn't about coercing women to be with him. They were either game or they weren't. He had no problems whatsoever accepting a no the first time around. Though he would certainly be lying if he said a no from her wouldn't disappoint him more than most.

"Do you have a place to shower in that one-room cottage of yours?"

He nodded slowly, like if he was approaching one of his horses.

"Yes," he replied. The bright smile on her face told

him he needn't have worried about her being as skittish as a colt. The sparkle in her eye was bold, brilliant and confident. She was definitely game. However, he still waited to hear the words.

"Give me first dibs on the shower and you've got a deal."

He let his eyes slide down her bent form, his better judgment screaming at him that this was a mistake he couldn't afford to make. With ease, he tuned out the sound until it was all but gone. Because there was one thing he knew—however they spent their time tonight, whether it was talking or burning up the sheets, he was not going to miss out on the opportunity to spend the night with Keely Tucker.

"It's a deal."

Twelve

"God that was amazing."

Jacob looked up from the food fixings he'd kept surrounded by ice packets in his saddlebags and time stopped when his gaze landed on Keely. The outposts were stocked with food and clothing for any hands that might find themselves stuck out here unexpectedly.

They kept unisex clothing that could be worn by any gender, so anyone who found themselves out here could comfortably remain huddled down here if need be.

Their offerings mostly comprised sweats, denims, flannel shirts and tees. And because they were gender neutral, they didn't exactly hang in a flattering manner from most bodies.

But Keely Tucker wasn't most bodies. He'd known that from the first time he'd met her. She was full-figured, sexy as hell and currently the object of his fixation as she sauntered out of the bathroom dressed in a pair of sweatpants and a baggy white tee that hung from one of her shoulders as if it was made to do so.

How she made that shapeless piece of cotton look like the sexiest piece of lingerie he'd ever seen, he didn't know. All he did know was that he was grateful for the kitchen counter standing between them. If he had to stand directly in front of her without any barriers, he might be tempted to do something stupid like pull her close to him so he could know how she fit against him and if that fit was just as decadent as he hoped it would be.

"What's for dinner? It smells amazing."

"Leftover ham. It's not a grand meal, but a little seasoning will take it from an average sandwich to something memorable."

She sat down on the opposite side of the small counter, her gaze focused directly on him. He shouldn't have been surprised to find her watching him. Keely was a designer. Her observational skills were probably better than most. But her gaze made him feel exposed in a way he couldn't ever remember, as if there was nothing he could hide from her, no matter how much he desired to.

He was a twenty-nine-year-old man, and he'd never experienced that kind of connection with someone where all his pretenses and defenses wanted to naturally lie down. He couldn't understand for the life of him why his brain decided Keely should be the one he felt comfortable enough to do so with.

"Everything okay?"

"Yeah," he replied. "I'm just feeling a bit antsy after all that physical labor. I'm gonna shower while the food finishes heating up in the oven. If I'm not back when the timer goes off, would you take it out of the oven for me?"

She nodded, and he headed into the bathroom. His brain might have decided Keely was the one to let down his guard with, but his instinct wouldn't let him do it. If it had, he might just have told her she was the most beautiful woman he'd ever come across, and her personality made him want to spend as much time as possible in her presence.

Old habits died hard and Jacob's habit of keeping women out was just too ingrained in him to just stop without consideration. He checked the food one last time before heading across the room to the shower.

Once the door was closed behind him, he made quick work of stripping and showering. Part of his haste was because he had food in the oven and burned ham wasn't something anyone with a decent palate wanted. The other part was that he knew what he wanted to happen tonight, and if he stayed in here too long, applying that obligatory consideration he'd been so dead set on a few moments ago, he might just talk himself out of this unspoken thing that was happening between him and Keely.

"Stop with the back-and-forth, Jacob. Just go out

there, share a meal with her and let things naturally evolve from there."

It had been so long since he'd done this dance with a woman, he felt awkward trying to execute the steps. Sex, he remembered. But this connecting with someone to get to the sex part didn't feel as simple as it used to.

His last girlfriend exited his life over a year ago. Since then, he'd indulged in a hookup or two, but Keely wasn't a woman who could be easily placed in the hookup category.

She wasn't forgettable. He'd certainly tried. But over the last few days she'd been here, she'd somehow managed to make her presence so noticeable, he was beginning to find it strange when she wasn't around.

"Stop frettin', Jacob."

Resigned to his new plan, he dressed quickly in much the same attire as Keely, except the garments didn't manage to look anywhere near as fashionable on him as they had her.

When he entered the room, she was standing at the counter, layering bread and the ham on plates.

"You didn't have to do that." She looked up at the sound of his voice, gifting that self-assured yet warm smile of hers.

"You've fed me for the last couple of nights and made sure I wasn't in the dark. The least I can do is make you a plate."

He sat down on a bar stool, feeling at a loss of what to do. At least when he was in the kitchen, he had the preparation of the food to keep him busy. But standing here as she moved gracefully around the small space, he had nothing else to do but look at her.

And looking at her was a problem, because every time he laid eyes on her, he wanted to break his own rules and learn more about her, making her more than just a random lay.

No matter how he wanted her, that was a risk he wasn't sure he could take. Not when he was so close to finalizing his dream of making the Slick Six the number one horse stable in the world.

When she was finished plating the sandwiches, she came around to his side of the counter and sat next to him. She wasn't touching him, but she was close enough that he could smell the store-brand vanilla shower gel in the bathroom wafting up from her skin. On him, it smelled like run-of-the-mill soap. On her, mixed with her particular body chemistry, it smelled like the most tantalizing thing he'd ever had the pleasure of experiencing.

"So, tell me how you got into the horse business. Is it like a family thing?"

He should've been relieved she was going for small talk. That was especially true since the topic was his business, the thing that had been his sole focus for the last eight years of his life.

"Yes and no. My parents were farmers. It provided a good living, but it was their passion so it never really seemed like work to them. That wasn't the case with me."

She took a bite of her sandwich and shared a sly

smile with him. "Let me guess, you thought you were too cute for all that? You needed to do something cooler like raise horses?"

He couldn't help but be amused by her easy way of saying whatever was on her mind.

"Something like that. Horses just always got me. I was a later-in-life child, so there weren't any other kids to play with. Horses always seemed to get me better than people. So, while my parents were farming, I was spending all my time with the few horses we had on the farm."

She watched him intently as he spoke, as if she was taking in every detail and committing it to memory.

"So, because you liked playing with the horses, you decided you were gonna be some sort of cowboy as an adult?"

"Honestly, that's every little boy's dream at some point," he replied. "But it wasn't that obvious to me."

He cracked open the water bottle she'd placed in front of him before she sat down and took a cool swig as he remembered that day.

"I just knew I liked horses as sort of a hobby. It never dawned on me that working with them could be a career. Then, when I was in college for business management, I went with a few friends to a horse show. A trainer was catching hell trying to get one of his more stubborn steeds to cooperate. I walked over and asked if I could try. I talked to the horse, showed him a little love, and he was literally eating out of the palm of my hand by the time it was all said and done.

“The trainer told me I should really think about going into horse training because I was a natural. That’s when the idea of training and possibly breeding horses became solidified in my head. I told my parents and they supported me. They allowed me to take a bit of their land and start with a few local horses here and there. The business took off. I did so well, soon I was bringing in more money than their farming. They allowed me to expand over the years, and when they retired a few years back, they gave me the business and told me to run with my dreams. Hence, the Slick Six Stables was born.”

When he looked up from his plate and turned to her, he expected to find her eyes glazed over with boredom. To his surprise, they were anything but. Her gaze was focused on him, as if she was fascinated by every word he spoke.

“That’s pretty impressive.” She cleared her throat, looking downward at her plate. “Both your tenacity and your parents’ support of your dream.”

Her voice was tinged with the slightest bit of melancholy that the average person probably wouldn’t have picked up on. But he realized he paid so much attention to Keely, even the slightest change in her made him sit up and take notice.

“You sound as if that’s…rare.”

He hedged his words. They hadn’t known each other long enough for him to be bulldozing his way into her past. But he wanted her to know that if she wanted to talk about it, whatever *it* was, he was interested in listening to her.

"It is. My parents were not supportive of my dream."

He couldn't help but raise both brows in surprise. People who were as bold and confident as Keely was often had a host of people behind them telling them they were the best at everything. It never would've occurred to him she didn't have the support of anyone who came into her orbit.

She paused for a bit before she returned her gaze to his and continued. "My parents were great parents. They loved my sister and I to pieces. It's just, we grew up really poor. We lived in the projects." She took a sip from her bottle of water as if she needed a moment to gather herself. "I'm not sure if you know what that is down here, but it's low-income housing. In New York, they're dark, dank apartment buildings that resemble prisons more than someone's domicile."

He was familiar. His family wasn't so far removed from their humble beginnings that he was completely ignorant of the topic. In Texas, the Housing Authority looked like cookie-cutter shacks rather than the high-rise brick-and-metal monstrosities Keely was speaking of.

"My parents struggled a lot until they were finally able to scrape enough together to put my mom through nursing school. Once she got a job, my dad went to school and became an X-ray tech. Once he finished school and started working, he went on to medical school and became a radiologist."

Jacob could see the pride she held in her parents as her eyes lit up with awe and her cheeks sat high on her face as her wide smile bloomed across her lips.

"The medical field literally took us from the projects to a four-bedroom house in Washingtonville just before I started high school. Their choices gave us security. So, listening to their teenage daughter talking about how she wanted to go to fashion school instead of doing something practical like going to school or getting a good civil job, it didn't really compute for them."

Context truly was everything. "So, they weren't being unsupportive, just cautious and concerned. They couldn't see beyond their limited experience."

Her brow pinched into a deep V as her eyes locked with his.

"You're the first person I've ever told that story to who understood their perspective. I love my parents and they love me. They were just deathly afraid I'd end up unable to support myself. They understood what that felt like and wanted more for me."

He could understand that, especially after learning how they'd used their education in a practical field to pull their family out of poverty.

"So how did you get around their restrictive thinking?"

"Before they would pay for me to go to FIT, that's Fashion Institute of Technology."

He raised a hand. "I'm not that country that I don't know what FIT stands for."

She gave a quick nod before continuing. "I had to complete a twelve-month LPN course—"

He held up his hand again. "Okay, I'm not so familiar with that acronym."

Her smile bloomed into full-on laughter. When she was able to get a hold of herself again, she picked up where her story had stopped.

"LPN stands for Licensed Practical Nurse. In addition to earning it, they demanded I get and hold a part-time job in a medical facility or doctor's office while I attended FIT. They wanted to make sure I had the education and work experience necessary to fall back on if my fashion dreams didn't pan out."

"That's some serious parenting right there." It might not have been the route his parents had chosen to go, but he definitely saw the value in the path Keely's parents had chosen.

"It really was. Although I didn't love being an LPN, the money I saved while working and going to school helped me create a nice little nest egg that became my start-up money for my stylist business. I can't say I was happy about their stipulations to begin with, but in the end, I couldn't really be mad."

"And do they accept your decision now?"

"They do. But I can tell they still worry that there's no stability in my chosen profession. I think that's the worst part of it. That thing in their eyes that says they're worried about me. It's why I've worked so hard. I need to make sure this works for me and for them. I don't want them to worry. That means I can't fail."

He felt that determination in his soul. He understood the drive to guarantee success no matter what. That need had dogged him since his parents gave him his first opportunity. He knew what a gift it was and he refused to squander it.

"There's nothing wrong with being determined, Keely. I'm sure your parents are very proud."

"They are." She turned slowly to him, scanning his face for something he couldn't exactly name. Maybe it was understanding and commiseration. Perhaps it was comfort. Whatever it was, it made him lean in closer than he should have.

"You're right, there's nothing wrong with being driven. It just doesn't leave room for much else in your life. It leaves you…"

"Lonely."

He could see the surprise in her eyes that he would understand. But every time he sat down to talk to her, he realized he understood her a whole lot more than most people around him.

"Don't be so surprised. The other night when you thought you'd offended me by talking about how lucky the women in my life must be, I wasn't offended. I was just reminded that no woman would ever have that luxury because my work always comes first."

She leaned in a little closer as if she was trying to soak up every word he spoke. Like maybe she'd been waiting for someone to speak words like this to her. He wouldn't find it so strange if she were. He certainly never thought he'd find a woman who understood why work had to be first.

"All the women I've dated since I've started this place say they understand my determination. But after a handful of cancellations because something work-related comes up, they're either complaining about my neglect or writing me off altogether. I just got tired of it and decided I should probably just stick to being alone."

"So, there's been…"

"Hookups," he answered. "There've been hookups. But there hasn't been anyone I could sit around having a laugh with or someone I could talk to about how demanding my work is. There's been no one I could really look forward to getting to know because most women I encounter haven't dealt well with my absence in the relationship."

She gently placed her hand on his thigh, using it to steady herself as she leaned closer into his space. Their lips were close enough to touch save for the thin sliver of space just big enough for air to slip between them.

"And what if you found someone who was just as career-focused as you? Someone who couldn't afford the distraction of a relationship, but would really love the chance to get to spend some time with a man that respected her work ethic and didn't need her constant attention to feel validated. Would you be willing to indulge in a friends-with-benefits situation-ship if you found a woman like that?"

Her voice was sultry, its deep tones sending jolts of

electricity up his skin that were so enticing, he could already feel his cock twitching in his very revealing, very loose sweatpants. He watched her brow rise in anticipation as she waited for his answer. And when she allowed the pink tip of her tongue to slide across those full lips of hers, there was only one answer he could utter.

"Hell yeah."

Thirteen

She'd only intended to press her lips lightly against his to seal the bargain they'd just agreed to. Somehow, the peck she'd intended morphed into something needy and hot once her flesh touched his.

The fire poured from his lips to hers, spilling inside her, spreading through her, consuming her until she thought she just might turn to ash right there. But then she felt his large hands move confidently up her thighs, moving on to her hips, curling his fingers into the fabric there, pulling her toward him.

She went willingly. There was no way in hell she was going to miss out on getting closer to him, of feeling the hard planes of his body that she was sure had been carved in the very fields they'd ridden through earlier.

He deepened the kiss, tightening his hold on her, splaying his tree-trunk thighs wide and pulling her between them, letting one of his hands dip to that sensitive spot in the small of her back. If she let this continue, if his fingertips made their way under her shirt, touching her there, she'd be lost.

She pulled away from him, moaning as the sweet ache of need coursed through her veins, begging her to reconnect her mouth with his.

"You are very good at that." She trembled in disbelief as the unrecognized huskiness in her voice rent the air.

"I am very good at a lot of things, sugah."

The cockiness in his hushed tone was as much of a turn-on as his searing mouth and blistering touch. Men who bragged of their sexuality never did it for her. But somehow, she knew that Jacob wasn't boasting. Everything from the certainty in his tight embrace to the sure way he pressed his lips against hers confirmed he was going to deliver on everything that hard, big body of his was promising her.

"I can see that. But are you sure you really wanna do this? I mean, someone who guards his freedom and privacy as much as you do, I don't know if you really understand what you're getting yourself into."

She allowed her hands to slide down the corded muscles of his arms until her fingers were covering his at the small of her back.

"Why don't you come a little closer, and I'm certain you'll understand just how interested I am in your proposition." He pulled his full bottom lip between his teeth, taunting her to give in. And she wanted to give in. But Keely was in Royal for a reason. No matter how tempted she was by her sexy host, she had to make certain they were both aware what they were agreeing to. She couldn't afford to lose sight of what her goal was.

"I'm serious, Jacob. I need to know you can agree to this just being for fun. No catching feelings. Neither of us has time for that."

"Are you really worried I don't know what I want?"

She took in the sight of him, his mouth curled into a cocky grin, the muscles in his thighs flexing and his cock, long and thick against her as he kept her caged between his legs.

"I think it's pretty obvious you know what you want in this moment. But my concern is maybe your eyes are getting too big for your belly."

"Are you asking me if I can handle you?"

He placed his hands on her hips, tugging her toward him. His grip was firm enough to keep her right where he wanted her but loose enough that if she truly wanted to free herself from him, she could.

"No." She looked him directly in the eyes, making sure he knew she was serious about what she was preparing to say. "I'm trying to make sure you can really accept who I am and what my focus is. I've had men tell me before they can handle keeping it easy. But sooner or later, they catch feelings, and then get upset when work is my priority. I can't lose sight of what I'm here for. I can't get mixed up in anything that's going to get in the way of me taking over the fashion design world."

He stood up, backing her up against the counter and confining her between his thick arms.

"Keely." The sound of her name on his lips shook something loose in her, something that had her wanting to scale this mountain of a man like professional climbers on Everest. "I'm a grown-ass man and I know how to entertain myself. It's not my expectation that you coddle me and keep me entertained."

He moved closer, pressing her into the counter as he leaned down, kissing along her jaw, until his lips were at the sensitive area of skin right underneath her ear.

"Now that we've got that outta the way, for the record, you also don't have to worry about me biting off more than I can chew. I'm a big boy and I like grown-man portions. I like my cut of meat tender." He punctuated the word with a kiss to her neck. "Browned to perfection." His lips traveled again until they were at the junction of her neck and shoulder, forcing a hard shiver of pleasure through her body. "And thick as all hell."

His lips touched just beneath her collarbone, making her body arch as if it were begging him to continue his journey downward. "If you're willing, I promise you, my appetite is more than hardy enough to appreciate exactly what you're offering."

He stepped back from her, letting his hungry gaze slide down the length of her, making her long for everything that heated stare promised her.

"So, are you ready to dine, or do you still need to check out the offerings?"

"I'm…ready."

His crooked smile returned right along with that brazen spark in his eye. He held out a meaty hand to her as he cocked his head to the side.

"Then come here, thickness."

The way that word rolled off his tongue made every cell in her body quiver with need and want, and desire so strong she could feel heat burning through her like molten lava through a Dixie cup. And without the slightest bit of hesitation, even though smart money said she should probably leave this sexy-ass man alone, Keely laced her fingers through his and eagerly followed him in the direction of the double bed against the far wall.

She made one stop on their way to the bed, pulling up next to the couch and grabbing her mini backpack to quickly search for the condom she usually kept in her wallet. When his brow furrowed, she rummaged around in a zipped compartment of the bag, smiling when she found the wallet and pulled out the foil packet she'd been looking for.

"Now." She winked at him, biting her bottom lip as she took in the full image of him with a very generous dick print behind his loose sweats. "Now we're ready."

Considering the short amount of time she would be in town, he naturally assumed that if he ever got the opportunity to have her body wrapped around him, it would be a one-off and he would take his time to savor the delicacy that was Keely Tucker. Apparently, he lied to himself, an emerging pattern he was beginning to notice where Keely was concerned.

From the moment she placed her hand in his and allowed him to lead her to the double bed, it was like a match to gasoline-soaked kindling. When he pulled her into his arms, and her lush body fit so perfectly against his, any designs he had on taking his time were out the window.

A fact that was spurred on by the hungry, needy sounds spilling from Keely's lips every time he held her tighter, or touched her.

He could get drunk off this woman. Presented with this opportunity, that's exactly what he planned to do.

Their clothes came off in a flustered hurry as they tried to navigate how to remain touching while needing to separate to undress. It was frantic and clumsy, but soon, Keely Tucker was standing before him naked, pulling him atop her as she lay across the bed like an all-powerful deity waiting to be worshipped by the unworthy commoner standing before her.

Would he ever be worthy of a woman like Keely? So self-assured, so in control of her own dreams that she was well on her way to building an empire. Probably not, but that didn't stop him from reaching for what he wanted either. And right now, more than shelter in bitter cold, more than cold water in a Texas heat wave, Jacob wanted Keely with his whole being, and he intended to have her.

The thought occurred to him that he should at least

try to curb his craven appetite, take things a little slower and give Keely time to adjust to what was happening between them.

But when he attempted to pull away, she wrapped those gorgeous, endless legs around him, locking her ankles, keeping him right where she apparently wanted him.

"We can do slow later. Need you now."

How had he gotten so lucky to stumble across this treasure of a woman? She was his match in so many things. It was as if they were living parallel lives. But what were the odds that she'd be just as desperate as he was to press their flesh together until they blended into one.

She tossed the condom at him, spreading her legs wider as he sat back on his haunches to sheathe himself. But as he tried to open the foil packet, he was distracted by the sight of Keely's fingers disappearing inside her body and all of his motor functions seized up.

In an instant, his cock went from hard to steel in just a matter of strokes. He growled, half enjoying watching her pleasure herself, but also jealous that it wasn't his fingers she was riding.

"Dammit, woman."

"I'd suggest you hurry up. I'm almost there."

With each roll of her hips and each dip of her fingers into her cavern, she was taunting him, daring him to join her or watch her bring herself to bliss. The message was clear. Either way she was going to get hers, and he'd be damned if that wasn't the sexiest thing he'd ever seen.

Determined not to miss out on much more, he found just enough focus to carefully remove the condom and quickly sheathe himself.

By the time she removed her fingers, now slick with her desire, and slid them between her folds, caressing her clit like he wanted to, he was ready to burst. He placed himself at her entrance, silently asking if she was still game for all of this. She reached down, wrapping him in the fingers she'd just used to pleasure herself, and that was all the confirmation he needed that she was still on board with the plan. And in his mind that plan was to get each other off as hard and fast as they could, hopefully without injury.

He pressed in until her warmth was completely surrounding him, taking a moment to get a handle on his senses that were screaming with excitement.

"Move, dammit." Her face was contorted in a strange mix of need and satisfaction, and he took her biting words as a compliment.

"God you're so pushy."

"Like you don't love it," she replied, and he couldn't deny it. He was loving every second of this experience so far.

Determined to give them both what they wanted, he set out a punishing pace that had her quivering around him. She was squeezing him so tight, he knew it was only a matter of time before she reached her peak.

He grabbed her hips, changing the angle of his stroke

just so, and without hesitation, her body spasmed, tensing around him as she climaxed beneath him.

Watching her fight her way through such a powerful release made fire burn in his veins.

"That's it, darlin', give in, let me have what I want."

Yes, he was one of those men who got off on knowing he could get women off, and he didn't even have the decency to be the slightest bit ashamed of it. Watching her be consumed by the pleasure he gave her, it was the headiest aphrodisiac he'd ever felt and if he could, he'd keep her like this, coming on his cock, wild and brazen beneath him, forever.

His traitorous body vetoed that idea as he felt his own climax climbing up his spine. His rhythm faltered as he tightened his grip on Keely's hips, anchoring himself lest he lose complete control. And when she wrapped her legs around him again, keeping him pressed against her, he gave in to the temptation to let go.

His orgasm ripped through him, causing him to falter, losing his grip and collapsing against her. She wrapped her whole body around his, planting sweet kisses along his neck as she rubbed his back and spoke to him in soft words.

"Shh, I got you, Jacob."

And she certainly did. There wasn't a force on earth that could cause him to relinquish this precious space in her body that she'd so graciously gifted him with nor the comfort he found in her arms. There was only one problem that he could think of as the orgasmic fog began to clear his head.

Now that he knew what she felt like in the throes of passion, what her flesh felt like pressed against his, Jacob wasn't certain he could let this go when the time came. And it would. He knew that with a certainty. It would come.

Fourteen

Keely sat at a table in the rear of the Royal diner, waiting for her guest to arrive. As she sipped on her coffee, the dark, sleeping screen of her iPad mini mocked her idleness. There was a time when every free moment she had would be spent on this device, sketching, arranging her business schedule or jotting down ideas for things future Keely should take care of. Not today, however. Today, she'd been sitting at this table for at least twenty minutes reliving every moment of her time in Jacob Chatman's bed.

She shook her head at the irony of her drilling Jacob about his acceptance of the no-distractions rule when she sat here unable to abide by said rule herself.

Keely girl, it was one night. It's not like you've never had sex before.

Yes, she'd certainly indulged before. But never to the point where she'd been so desperate for another taste that she'd had to fight herself to get out of bed and make it to her meeting on time.

If only it were just last night, though.

If it was only about their one shared night together, maybe she could eventually put that out of her mind and focus. But anticipation of their date tonight made her a little too eager to get back to the Slick Six Stables and Jacob Chatman in the bold, living flesh.

Not the time, Keely. Not the time.

She glanced up at that moment to see Rylee Meadows, Ariana's wedding planner, step into the diner, and she knew it was time to shake off this post-coital fog clouding her head. The two women had only spoken once on a brief video chat, but Keely couldn't risk seeming flighty and unreliable because her senses were still overwhelmed by Jacob's ability to please her.

She took a large swallow of coffee, hoping the caffeine would jump-start her brain, before waving to catch Rylee's attention.

"It's so nice to finally meet you in person, Keely."

Keely stood, extending her hand to the young woman when she finally stood at Keely's table.

"Same," Keely offered. "I can't wait to talk about some of the ideas you have. I'll be meeting with the florist and caterer later in the week to see how we can incorporate touches from the dress into the floral arrangements and the food."

Rylee sat down opposite Keely and pulled out her

laptop. Setting it up quickly, she pulled up a list of ideas and sample pictures for Keely to peruse.

"Ariana talked about doing an Old Hollywood theme for the wedding decorations." Rylee pointed to the screen for Keely to follow along. "I was thinking we could use cream, gold and black to really amp up that elegance factor."

"That's gorgeous," Keely responded. "I like the idea about the Hollywood glam. In fact, Ariana's choice of dress design fits perfectly with that. The only problem is she's decided she wants to add a little bit of Texas into the dress design to represent Ex's home state."

Keely swiped her fingers across her tablet until she found the picture she was looking for.

"I had the idea that we could incorporate the bluebonnet, the Texas state flower, into her dress. As you can see here, it's a bluish-purplish color. The gold and the cream might coordinate well with that. I'm just not sure the combo of gold, cream and black will work."

"Hmm." Rylee twisted her mouth to the side as she looked back and forth between her laptop screen and Keely's tablet. As a fellow creative, Keely recognized that look—it meant Rylee was running down all the configurations and combinations of the aforementioned colors to see if she could come up with a solution. "I see what you mean. How about if we toss the black as you suggest and use gold as the primary color, the bluish-purplish color as the secondary and the cream as the tertiary? I think those three would make a striking trio. Could you make that work with her dress?"

"Absolutely," Keely replied. "Her dress is made from an antique white satin. I'm toying with adding color to the piping for a subtle yet vivid accent. Hopefully the florist will be able to procure enough bluebonnets for the bouquets, boutonnieres and the venue decorations."

Keely looked up and saw a light spark in Rylee's eyes. It was the result of collaboration between creatives when their ideas came together into a beautiful explosion.

"This is going to be amazing." Rylee's excitement was contagious, and soon Keely was feeling like her normal, focused self. It was a relief to feel some of her usual dedication to detail and determination filter back into her system. This was what she was in Royal for, to make Ariana's dress the linchpin of the wedding of the century. And if the excited way Rylee was tapping away at her laptop keys was any indication, Keely was halfway to accomplishing her goal.

See what you're capable of when your mind is on the right things?

Yeah, she saw. But as a memory from the previous night in that outpost tried to claw its way back to the surface of her mind, she had to wonder if keeping her head screwed on right would be as easy as reminding herself of her purpose. Because right now, the only purpose her head wanted to acknowledge was how she would purposely enjoy stripping that man naked and running her tongue over every inch of his glorious skin.

Rylee chose that moment to look across the table at Keely with a concerned look in her eyes.

“Are you all right, Keely? You seem a bit flushed.”

She was flushed all right. But since there was no way in hell Keely could tell Rylee the truth about what had her blood rushing through her vessels right now, she waved her hand in front of her face and said, “It’s this Texas heat.” She dropped back against her chair and grabbed the tepid glass of water the waitress had provided twenty minutes ago when Keely first arrived. “I guess it’s turning out to be more than I bargained for.”

“Well, good morning to you, sunshine.”

Jacob walked into the stables with a travel cup of coffee in his hand. It was closer to afternoon than morning and he was just beginning his workday. He knew he was supposed to feel bad about that, but after spending all night buried deep inside Keely’s warmth, there was no way he could give a good goddamn about the flogging his foreman was about to give him.

He and Keely had gotten precious few hours of sleep before they headed back from the outpost at the first rays of dawn. He was supposed to get dressed and head out to work, but watching her curled up in his bed as she found her way back to the land of nod had proved too tempting for him to resist. He’d lain down behind her, just to embrace her nearness for a few seconds—or at least that was the lie he told himself at the time. The next thing he knew he’d woken up to the sun high in the sky and a folded note explaining she’d gone into town where Keely’s warm body had once been.

"I know, I know," he said with as much vigor as a man tired from having amazing sex all night long could muster. "I'm late. But I'm here now, so let's get on with our day."

"You rib me if I'm only fifteen seconds early to my post." Matt's raised brow and amused smile entertained more than annoyed Jacob. A result he could only attribute to his night with Keely putting him in such a good, relaxed mood. "You know I can't let the fact slide that you're more than a couple of hours late."

"You wouldn't be Matt if you did."

Matt nodded his agreement and turned to Jacob, smiling like he was in on a secret no one else knew.

"I couldn't help but notice your guest didn't come down until late this morning too. What exactly were you two doing at that outpost last night?"

"We played chess," Jacob offered with a straight face, not caring one bit if his friend believed him. That was his story and he was sticking to it.

"Chess," Matt echoed. "That's what we're calling it now?"

"I know I pay you to do more than get on my nerves."

Matt nodded. "You do. But getting on your nerves is a job perk I plan to take full advantage of."

Jacob couldn't help but chuckle at that. Matt's antics had been Jacob's only source of entertainment for so long, he had to admit it would be strange if all the man did was do his job without giving Jacob crap every chance he got.

"Have the new arrivals been assigned to their trainers yet?"

Matt grabbed a nearby clipboard and handed it to Jacob.

"Yeah. The staff has been briefed and they've already met their new charges. Also, while you were taking your time getting here, I took a call this morning from Ezra Stanley, the owner of a world champion horse. Apparently, he isn't too happy with his current trainer and is interested in talking to you about bringing his horse down to the Slick Six for training for the next round of qualifying events."

Jacob's jaw dropped open as he took in what Matt was saying. This wouldn't be the first prize-winning horse the Slick Six had trained. But a medal winner? That was gold right there as far as word-of-mouth advertising. If Jacob and his staff could make this owner happy, he'd have the hype to his reputation he needed to pull bigger and definitely more lucrative contracts.

"Hot damn," Jacob yelped, the sharp sound drawing out a loud bark of laughter from Matt. Both men knew there wasn't too much that could get Jacob this excited. He was solemn and serious on his best day, ornery and grumpy on his worst. This was damn near euphoria where Jacob was concerned.

"Hold on, big man. He wants to schedule a visit out here to take a look at our facilities and meet our training staff before he makes his decision. I told him you'd call him back with the schedule after you met with the staff."

Jacob nodded, so thrilled, all the fatigue he'd walked

into the stables with was now replaced by a jolt of adrenaline.

"Tell the staff we're having an emergency meeting now. Wherever they are on the property, they need to be in the conference room at the main house ASAP. We've got a world champion to court."

He turned around, leaving the stables and heading straight for the house. This was just the chance he'd been waiting for and finally, after so many years of backbreaking labor, he was about to get the chance of a lifetime.

He made it to the house in what seemed no time. He made quick work of getting the conference room ready. Despite dropping everything he touched at least twice, he still managed to get the space set up before his staff arrived.

Too full of energy, he couldn't sit still, so he paced back and forth, hoping to burn off some of these excitement jitters he just couldn't seem to shake.

"Jacob… Jay… Are you home?"

Jacob stopped moving the second he heard Keely's voice traveling through his halls. The sound of her rich alto soothed his need to be in motion. Eager to see her, but pressed for time since he knew his staff would be converging on the house soon, Jacob didn't stop to wonder why the moment he heard her voice calling his name, everything inside him stilled in a way even a soothing cup of rum-spiked coffee couldn't have managed.

When he found her in the kitchen, he didn't stop to speak. He simply planted his hands on her waist, pulled her until she was pressed against him in the most delicious way and locked his mouth to hers.

The sweet mewling sounds she made while he nibbled at her bottom lip was pure addiction, a sound he wanted to hear over and over as many times as she'd allow him to hear it. But as much as he enjoyed the taste of her, unless he wanted to share all their business with his employees, he had to find some decorum and set her free.

"Well, that was a very lovely greeting. What did I do to deserve that?"

He pulled her hips toward him again, loving the feel of her pressed so tightly against him.

"I am celebrating some feel-good news. And since you spent all night making me feel good, I thought it was appropriate I share it with you first."

She lifted her eyes to the ceiling while her coy smile lit up a flame in his chest that was growing brighter and brighter each time he encountered her.

"I did put a lot of work into making you feel good last night, didn't I?"

"You certainly did," he agreed, taking the opportunity to steal another kiss while they were still alone. "Also, you left me alone in bed. Since I also put in a lot of work too, I think I deserve a sweet treat as well."

She nodded, easily agreeing with his recollection of events. "Hard work like ours deserves to be rewarded."

"True," he replied. "So, sit down and let me tell you my news so we can both be rewarded."

She stepped out of his embrace and hopped up on

one of the stools at the counter in the center of the kitchen.

"Don't keep me guessing, man. What happened?"

"Today, we got an inquiry from the owner of a medal-winning horse. He's interested in bringing his horse here to start training for the next quals season. He wants to come down and tour the place, and check out my trainers to see if the Slick Six is as good as our reputation claims we are."

He watched her eyes grow wide and her jaw drop in surprise, and it was as if something inside him clicked for the first time that he couldn't understand.

"Jacob, I don't know a thing about horses," she spoke in a rushed, excited cadence. "But even I can see how huge an opportunity this is. Congratulations."

Her exuberance over his accomplishment made him want to yank her close to him again. No other woman he'd been romantically involved with could give a damn about hearing about his work. He understood it. He didn't have one of those sexy jobs like corporate CEOs and the like. His work was dirty, backbreaking and, most of all, time-consuming. There weren't too many women he'd come in contact with who wanted to know anything about what he did.

But seeing Keely celebrate with him, even though this opportunity didn't have a thing to do with her and there was no way for her to benefit from it, softened something in him, making him ache to keep her closer for a while longer. But just as soon as the thought crossed his mind, he realized the other half of the news he had to share with her. Suddenly, his good mood began to fade as he prepared for what had been the start of many arguments in the past.

"I'm about to hold a staff meeting to hammer down the logistics of this visit so I can put in a call to the owner before close of business today. That pretty much means I'll be unavailable for most of the day and probably part of the night."

She watched him carefully, understanding dawning in her eyes. He could tell the moment she realized what he was getting at and he braced himself for the usual antics he'd experienced whenever he had to cancel plans with a woman before.

"Jacob, don't worry about us going out tonight. This is way more important than you showing me around Royal. We had a deal, remember?" She waved her hand back and forth between them. "This can never get in the way of work. This is a huge opportunity. You can't half-ass it because you're hanging out with me when you should be handling your business. I wouldn't let you do it even if you tried."

Damn, just when he thought he had things figured out, here comes this woman turning him and his world upside down.

He stood there staring at her because he wasn't quite sure what to say. So many times, a moment like this would blow up into a tense fight about how he was neglecting the woman he was seeing. It was such a frequent occurrence he honestly didn't know how to respond to how well Keely was taking the cancellation of their first proper date.

The sound of worn cowboy boots on wood steps shook him out of his stupor. He glanced at Keely again.

"How did I get so lucky to find a friend as wonderful as you?"

She shrugged. "Truly, I don't know because I am pretty great."

She was. Even with her not so humble brag, they both knew she was telling the truth.

He stepped closer, taking a peek out the window to make sure they didn't have any spectators before he pressed a quick kiss to her smiling lips.

"You really are," he agreed.

"Glad you know it," she countered. "And if you go take care of work like the dedicated horse trainer I know you are, I'll make sure to reward all your hard work when we're the only two people in the house tonight."

"Is that right?"

She nodded her reply, and not for the first time, Jacob wondered how different his dating life might've been if he'd had an understanding partner like Keely.

"It certainly is, Mr. Chatman. Now go'n and get that bag."

Jacob took in the special woman standing before him, tipping his imaginary Stetson as he gave her an enthusiastic "Yes, ma'am."

She was gorgeous, creative and smart as all hell. But the thing he was most enamored with at this moment was how much she was like him when it came to dedication to work. Keely was proving to be a woman of her word by pressing him to take care of his business. She was also making it abundantly clear that she was the total package, every man's dream. And if he wasn't careful, he might just find himself falling for her.

Fifteen

Keely stepped away from her travel sewing machine, stretching the kinks out of her back and moving her fingers to get the circulation flowing in them again. Once she'd left Jacob to take care of his staff meeting, she'd locked herself away in the great room working on Ariana's train. The starlet wanted a detachable train that she could remove at the reception so she could party like the movie star she was.

In response to Ariana's request, Keely had designed a grand cathedral train that would've made the former Hollywood actress the late Princess Grace of Monaco jealous.

It was made of two panels. The first created the outer silhouette with a scallop lined of appliqué that perfectly matched the bluish-purplish color of the bluebonnet. The second panel was inset with the matching lace and chiffon of the sheer arms of the dress, speckled with tiny, hand-sewn, satin replicas of the flower's petals in the bluebonnet color. Now that the panels were sewn together, there was six feet of glamorous detachable train Keely was certain Ariana was going to be ecstatic about.

Keely stood in the middle of the room with her hands on her waist in a mock superhero pose. Considering how sluggish and unfocused she was at the start of the day, she was proud of how she'd managed to turn things around and make the day productive. She'd even managed to schedule meetings with the florist and the caterer next week so she could finalize Ariana's dress design once she saw some of the bouquet samples the florist would bring and the signature dishes the caterer would provide to accent the color scheme of the wedding.

There were still a couple of hours before the sun would begin to set, so she decided a quick trip into Royal proper for some supplies would be the best use of her time.

She found her way easily back to Main Street, taking in the quaint setting of what was probably one of the busiest streets in Royal. It was definitely the "city" part of town, but unlike some metropolises such as New York or LA, there was still a mindfulness to the atmosphere that major streets in larger cities didn't possess.

Keely parked at one end of the shopping area, hoping to peruse the storefront windows to figure out exactly what she was looking for. The sidewalks weren't crowded like in New York and she had to wonder if that was just the way of life here in Royal or if the blackout was keeping most people off the street.

As she walked by, she only saw a handful of shops with "Closed" signs hanging in their windows. Again, she didn't know if they were already closed for the day, or if they were still dealing with issues from the blackout. After everything that had happened between her and Jacob, she couldn't deny this blackout had the power to turn lives upside down. That was certainly the truth when it came to hers.

The sight of a candle shop with the lights on drew her in and before she knew it, she was entering the shop, taking in its soothing decor and aroma.

A smiling young woman with jet-black curls and blue eyes greeted Keely from behind the counter.

"I'm Jen. Welcome to Flicker. How can I help you today?"

Keely continued to look around as she made her way to the counter where Jen was standing.

"I'm so glad you were open. I was worried most of the stores might still be affected by the blackout. As soon as I saw your lights on, I knew I had to come in."

She saw the young woman's face soften with gratitude, sprinkled in with compassion. "I think most of the businesses are fine. Some are just closed down because people are waiting at home to deal with whatever issues losing power caused them. And with the advent of PayPal, Venmo, Cash App and card swipers that can attach to your cell phone or your iPad, most vendors are able to make sales without needing to plug in an old-fashioned cash register."

Keely could certainly commiserate. As uneasy as she was about staying with Jacob in the beginning, she'd at least been lucky enough to have a roof over her head and power at her disposal. Not everyone in Royal fared so well.

That gratitude over her circumstances was part of the reason she was here. Jacob had done something kind for her by letting her stay in his home, and she wanted to return the favor by doing something nice for him after his long but productive day.

Keely took a long sniff of the mixtures of scents and knew she was in the right spot. "It looks and smells wonderful in here." She could pick out berries, vanilla and lavender among the varied aromas. "I don't know how I'm going to make a selection."

Jen chuckled as if she'd heard this very same thing from every customer who'd walked through the shop's doors.

"Well, that's what I'm here for. Tell me who and what the candle is for, and I'll try to recommend some scents based on that."

The image of Jacob's marble-like body surrounded by water and the soft glow of candles brought a smile to her face. Jen must have picked up on Keely's expression, because without the slightest bit of hesitancy or discomfort, the woman matched Keely's grin.

"So, we're looking to set a romantic mood, are we?" Keely nodded and Jen continued. "Does your intended have more masculine or feminine energy?"

Keely thought about Jacob and tried to place his energy. "He definitely taps into the masculine. He loves physical labor, dirt and animals. But he does have this softer, nurturing side too. You see it when he cooks for the people around him or when he's caring for animals. Do you have anything for someone like that?"

"Sure do," Jen replied. "I think something like a sandalwood with a splash of vanilla could work for someone like that. It's a great combination of both masculine and feminine energies. I just made a fresh batch about forty-eight hours ago. They should be perfect now."

Jen waved her over to the back display wall, grabbing a squat candle in an elegant glass jar. She opened the cap, and handed it to Keely. "Do you think this will work?"

Keely brought the jar to her nose and moaned at the warm and woody scent wafting into the air.

"Definitely." Keely's excited answer broadened Jen's friendly smile. "I'll take as many as you have."

"Sure, it will take about fifteen minutes to get them packaged. Are you okay with that time frame?"

Keely gave a nod and walked over to the counter to complete the transaction. "I'll just continue browsing your shop in the meantime."

"Well, since you're my largest-selling purchase today, I'll add a little something special to your package." Jen gestured for Keely to follow her to a shelf to the right of the candles where she saw a huge oil display. She handed Keely a bottle and encouraged her to smell it.

"This is my best-selling product. It's a light massage oil that makes the skin silky smooth. You can add essential oils to it to make the most delightful fragrances if you choose. Since you like the sandalwood and vanilla, I'm thinking I could mix some of that up in the massage oil for you as a freebie in the candle basket."

Keely clapped her hands together like an excited child. "Free-ninety-nine is my favorite price." She might be able to afford luxury items with the huge come-up in her earnings, but Keely loved a bargain as well as a small business owner who offered small touches like this to make a client feel special.

Jen rung up the sale, her generous smile making Keely feel right at home. "I hope you love everything. By the looks of it, this is for a special occasion."

Keely stopped for a moment, realizing Jen was right. This was a special occasion. She intended to enjoy Jacob and all his wonderful touch had to offer, and considering the dry spell she'd had in both good company and good sex, *that*, along with celebrating Jacob's new opportunity, made tonight very special indeed.

But somehow, her plans ran so much deeper than the physical. She realized this wasn't just about the anticipated outcome, it was also about getting to share something with a man she was beginning to care for more than it was safe for her to admit.

When Jen informed her that her order was ready, she took her bags and headed out the store. As she stood on the sidewalk watching people mill by, it struck her as odd that the world around her was just running its normal course. She, on the other hand, was primed to have a partial existential crisis about what was happening between Jacob and her.

She took in a long, slow breath, allowing a calm smile to spread across her lips as she quieted her thoughts.

"Just keep it chill, Keely, and everything will be fine. Don't make it more than it has to be."

Jacob entered the back door to see all the lights turned out in the kitchen except the one over the stovetop. It left the room in a soft, warm glow that felt more inviting than usual.

Most nights when he came in late, he stayed in the kitchen long enough to grab something light to eat before he showered and headed to bed. But the adrenaline from all the plans he and his team had made today for the world champion's owner still had excitement buzzing through him.

In a week's time, Ezra Stanley would be visiting the Slick Six and, if everything went right, Jacob's plan to expand his business would finally get underway. He wanted to celebrate, and he wouldn't allow himself to feel the least bit bad that Keely was the only one he wanted to share this good time with.

Hoping she was still up, he took the back stairs two at a time and walked down the long quiet hallway until he reached the center, where the door to the master bedroom awaited.

He opened the door gently. He might be excited as hell, but he didn't want to startle Keely if she'd already fallen asleep. But when he stepped inside and swept his gaze from one side of the room to the next, the only thing he found were two candles, one on each nightstand, gently flickering.

"Keely?"

"In here," she called out, making him turn toward the en suite bath. The lights were turned down here as well, candles acting as the only source of light here too. His eyes swept across the vanity, to the large shower stall, and then finally to the huge Jacuzzi tub at the far end of the room.

There she was, leaning back against the porcelain, her head lolling against a bath pillow with her body submerged beneath water filled with suds and rose petals. One of her arms lay languidly against the edge of the tub, while the other was invisible underneath the suds.

He remembered when he'd had the master suite renovated, the interior designer and the contractor had practically twisted his arm to agree to installing that big thing. The truth was, in all the years he'd had it, he'd never actually used it. But the cost and the maintenance were all worth it just to glimpse this goddess looking like sin and temptation.

The golden-brown skin of her face, shoulders and neck seemed more bronzed in the dim candlelight, making him want to touch her even more. But when a soft moan escaped her lips and he watched her pull her submerged hand from the water before letting it slide down her neck, then chest and then lower, while her gaze locked with his, he thought he was going to combust right there on sight.

"Do you need a formal invitation, or are you gonna get your tail in here and join me?"

The lustful spark in her eyes dared him to respond. And he would. Just not verbally. Words wouldn't do right now. Action was what they both needed and he didn't plan to hesitate one moment longer.

Without a word, he shucked his clothing, then stepped in the opposite direction of the tub toward the shower. He'd spent most of his day in the conference room, but he'd still gone to the stables. And while he didn't mind the familiar scent of horses, he didn't want to taint the atmosphere Keely had obviously gone through the trouble of creating for him, so he took a quick shower, keeping the water as cool as he could stand it, because his only purpose was to get clean under the spray so he could get as dirty as he wanted in those suds with Keely.

Refreshed, he stepped out of the shower and headed straight for the tub. Dripping from head to toe, he didn't bother with grabbing a towel. His only focus was getting to the woman who had him harder than he'd ever been, and he hadn't touched her yet.

She greeted him with a wicked gleam in her eye that promised so much satisfaction, he quickly stepped into the tub, sloshing water over the sides and not giving a damn about the mess he was surely going to have to clean up later.

"Come here, you."

He settled behind her, pulling her back against his chest, sliding his hand down her lush sides and bringing them in front of her until his palms were cupping her heavy, luscious bosom.

"When you said you'd have a reward for me tonight, you weren't playing, huh?" He nuzzled her neck, placing a trail of soft kisses against her sizzling skin as she settled between his legs.

"I don't kid about my rewards, Mr. Cowboy. As hard as I work, I try to remember to play as hard too. Otherwise, I'll get burned out, and no one wants to deal with a burned-out Keely. She is decidedly not fun."

He kept one hand cupping her breast while the other traveled down her soft torso and abdomen until his fingers traced the top of her slick mound. She trembled in his arms and the vibrations brought a sly grin to his lips. This was only the beginning. By the end, he planned to have her breaking apart from his touch.

He slipped his fingers down to her folds, letting the edge of his fingertips tease the seam until she was canting her hips forward, proving just how much she wanted his touch.

"Mmm," she moaned deeply, gripping the sides of the bathtub for purchase when he grazed her sensitive button. "I'm supposed to be rewarding you." Her voice hitched as he pressed the pads of his fingers, stroking her clit in a painfully slow rhythm that she desperately wanted to chase.

"That's where you're wrong." He sped up his movements just slightly. "Feeling you pressed against me while my fingers commit every inch of your sex to memory." She tensed against him, rolling her hips underneath the water as he built up momentum. "That's the only reward I want right now."

He was telling the absolute truth. There was something about watching Keely come completely undone by his own hand that made him harder, hungrier for her than he could ever remember being.

Every twitch of her hips against him, his cock slid in between the crease of her bottom as if he was made to be there, and considering he was hard enough to cut glass at this moment, he was damn certain this was exactly where he belonged.

Keely spread her legs wider, giving him more room to work, planting her feet against the porcelain tub to give her more control in the water. He sped up his strokes, wrapping his open palm gently around the base of her neck, exposing the elegant line where her neck met her shoulder.

He licked a long, slow line from her shoulder, up her neck, until his mouth rested against her lobe. She trembled in his arms, her opening clasping at his fingers in desperation of the climax he gauged was just out of reach.

Jacob whispered cooing, soft sounds in her ear as

her pleasure-filled moans filled the dim room. Increasing the speed of his strokes, he kissed her lobe and smiled against the shell of her ear as he flicked his thumb against her hard nub.

"Let go, baby. Let me see you break apart for me."

Her body tensed and she keened, the sound so guttural and explosive, he could feel his heavy cock twitch against his stomach, begging for a release of his own.

She held on to the sides of the tub, bracing herself, as she splintered into tiny pieces, sloshing water over the sides. The water could flood the entire room for all he cared. The only thing he wanted was to witness the beauty of this woman shattering beneath his touch as he brought her to completion.

It may sound chauvinistic in today's world, and he'd probably never admit this aloud. But he had never felt more like a man than when he had this woman in his arms, falling to pieces from his touch.

And as she settled against him, her body still wracked with tremors as she tried to come down from her powerful climax, he knew for certain nothing in his future would ever compare to this.

When she recovered, she turned around on her knees, taking him in one hand while reaching to the side of the tub for the condom she'd placed there earlier. Once she had him sheathed, she slowly, almost painfully so, lowered herself over him, taking him into her warmth. And when she was completely seated, she leaned over him, kissing him deeply, before she leaned back, locking her sultry gaze with his, luring him into her web.

She knew she had him. He knew she had him, and by their mutual needy smiles, he figured they both were fine with that realization.

"It's my turn now," she murmured while rolling her hips in a slow, teasing pace. "Please, let me return the favor."

He spread his arms against the width of the tub and leaned back before whispering, "Be my guest."

"How did you come up with the name 'the Slick Six'?"

Jacob looked down to make sure he'd heard the sleepy voice tugging at the end of his consciousness. He wrapped an arm around Keely's waist and pulled her closer in his embrace. After their lovemaking escapade in the bathroom, they'd dried off, lotioned up and crawled under the covers of his king-size bed, slowly drifting into sleep in each other's arms.

"Now, why would you wanna hear a boring story like that? I guess I didn't put in enough work in that bathtub to tire you out if you need me to tell you a bedtime story."

She peered up at him with a lazy smile pulling at her full lips as she snuggled closer to him, entwining her legs with his.

"See that deflection tactic right there? That tells me that this is definitely a story I want to hear."

He leaned down, stealing a quick kiss before he spoke.

"Smart and sexy as hell. What have I even been doing with my life before you."

She smoothed her hand over his hip, gliding it along his skin, and then playfully pinching his backside.

"Yes, I am both those things. But you're still stalling. Get to talking, cowboy."

"Okay," he relented, realizing she wasn't going to drop the subject. "When I was a kid, my father introduced me to *Lone Ranger* reruns. And from that moment, everything in my life revolved around those characters. I didn't just love *The Lone Ranger.* I wanted to be the Lone Ranger."

He paused for a moment, remembering the joy he felt every time he sat down to watch his favorite show with his dad. That show was a seminal event in his young life, shaping his ideas of right and wrong.

"Well, when Halloween came along and my class was having a party, there was only one choice of a costume for me."

"I bet you were the cutest Lone Ranger too."

"My mama certainly thought so," he replied, laughing as he recounted how many pictures his mother had made him stand for before he could leave for school.

"When I got to the party, my classmates asked me if I was a sheriff or a regular cowboy. I told them neither, and proudly announced I was the Lone Ranger.

"Some of the kids didn't know who he was because they hadn't seen the show. But there was one boy there who was familiar and he yelled out, 'You can't be the Lone Ranger. You're Black and the Lone Ranger is white.'"

He could feel Keely flinch in his arms, as if she was trying to take the pain of that past blow for him. He smoothed a hand over her shoulder, calming her, letting her know he was all right.

"I don't think it bothered me so much when the kid said it because he was a kid. I figured there were people smarter than my fellow eight-year-olds. But what cut me was when my teacher, Mrs. Abernathy, agreed with him. Her saying it made it true. And when I made it home from school in tears, relaying what had happened, my parents were seething. But even though they were both hurt and angry for me, they set aside their feelings and set to figuring out a way to help me deal with what had happened."

She leaned up on her elbow, her gaze locked firmly on his as if she were completely invested in his tale. He didn't know why, but it was a source of comfort that she cared enough to listen.

"How'd they do that?"

"My dad, who absolutely hates the internet, got online and found a bunch of information about Black cowboys. Namely, that the Lone Ranger was actually based on a real-life Black cowboy named Bass Reeves, who was the first Black US Marshal. Learning that healed something in me that I hadn't realized the experience had tainted. It made me believe I could do, be anything, no matter what anyone else said.

"Bass Reeves, Bill Pickett, Isom Dart, Stagecoach Mary, Nat Love and Daniel W. Wallace, my dad looked at those six and said, 'Jacob—'" he thickened his Texas drawl to sound more like his father "'—these six cow-folk right here were slicker than a can of oil. They were innovative, and created the game. Everyone else is a pale imitation. Never let anyone's ignorance define who you are or who you want to be.'"

He couldn't help the warmth blooming through him as he remembered how great his father made him feel in that moment.

"I can see from your smile that what your dad did meant a lot to you."

"It really did," he replied. "It also didn't hurt when my mama went up to the school the next day and read my teacher the riot act and showed her how absolutely ignorant she was of actual history."

"So that's how you came up with the name, the Slick Six Stables?"

He nodded. "Yup. It's me paying homage to those the world has forgotten. Keeping their contributions to our history—" he moved a pointed finger back and forth between them "—American history, alive."

He wrapped a loose lock of her hair around his finger, loving how soft it felt against his skin. It was in that moment he realized it wasn't just her hair or any particular physical feature about her that was doing it for him. Well, not just that. It was also her presence. It was his ability to tell her something so personal, that only his parents knew that particular truth.

How this woman had found her way into the secret places of his mind, and if he were honest, his heart, he didn't know. What he was particularly aware of at this moment was that he liked it, and even though everything in him said he should fight this, all he wanted was to settle deeper into this feeling that Keely Tucker was stirring in him.

Sixteen

"What the hell, Matt?"

Jacob stalked toward his foreman just outside one of three training pens on the property. Matt visibly tensed at the barking sound of Jacob's voice while his eyes flickered back and forth rapidly as if he were trying to figure out what in the world Jacob was hollering his name for.

"Everything all right, boss?"

It was certainly a reasonable question in response to Jacob's displeased tone. As far as Jacob could remember, there weren't too many times in all the years Matt had worked with him that Jacob had found fault with the man. Especially nothing that warranted the kind of frustration currently running through him. But these weren't normal times. In two days, Ezra Stanley would be visiting Jacob's ranch to decide if he wanted to send his medal-winning horse to the Slick Six for preseason training.

As far as Jacob was concerned, that meant everyone on this ranch should be as jumpy and fixated on perfection as he was.

"Matt, I specifically asked you to take over lead trainer duties for the duration of Stanley's visit. You scheduled me instead. What's this all about?"

Matt loosened his shoulders a bit, relaxing his stance before sharing an amused grin with Jacob.

Since he found no humor in this situation at all, Jacob's annoyance ground harder against his nerves.

"I fail to see why you're laughing. You're the person I trust most on this ranch, Matt. If you're not in the pen when Stanley arrives, it could definitely impact whether he signs with us or not."

"Jacob." Matt said his name slowly, like he needed to make sure Jacob didn't miss a word of what he was about to say. "You didn't ask me to put myself down for training during the visit. You asked me to put your best trainer on the roster that day."

"Exactly," Jacob countered. "That's you."

Matt shook his head, confusing Jacob even further. "Jay, you are the best trainer the Slick Six has ever had. You know the ranch inside out because you built it from the ground up. You're a freakin' horse whisperer. No one can get these proud animals to respond like you do. Trust me, friend, you want Stanley to see you running things when he arrives, not me. You are the one who will sell the Slick Six. Not me."

Jacob stood back, taking in all his foreman, his friend, had said to him. It wasn't that Jacob didn't know he was good. He was damn good at his job. He'd broken his back to build this ranch into what it was. But now that he was on the cusp of getting everything he wanted, he suddenly had a case of the doubts.

"I'm sorry, Matt. I was out of line."

Matt chuckled, making Jacob's overreaction that much more prominent. "You were. But I won't hold it against you. You've been burning the candle at both ends since last week. It's got you rattled and tense. Maybe you should find a way to blow off some steam between now and then."

"No time."

Jacob shook his head, hoping to exaggerate the point. Matt was right about his not getting enough rest. He'd work his tail off all day and then spend his nights tangled up with Keely in his bed.

He wasn't complaining, not in the least. Having her around gave him an energy, a zeal he hadn't had since he'd first started the Slick Six. But his mood was definitely suffering from his lack of uninterrupted rest.

"I'm gonna finish up some admin work in the office. By the time I'm done, there will barely be enough time for a shower followed by dinner with Keely."

Jacob purposely left out the sex-with-Keely part. Matt didn't need to know all of his business.

"Dinner? Is that what we're calling it now? Because the way you two make eyes with each other whenever you're together, I'd figured there was a whole lot more than dinner going on at night."

"And just like that—" Jacob pointed a finger at his friend, fighting hard not to let truth permeate his expression "—you are once again the asshole in this situation."

"It's a gift, really." Matt placed a firm hand on Jacob's shoulder as his devious grin lit up his face. "You know what else is a gift?"

Jacob had no clue what Matt was going to say. There was no telling what would fly out of the man's mouth.

"No, but I'm sure you're gonna tell me."

Matt squeezed his shoulder, then pointed in the direction behind Jacob. "That beautiful woman walking this way with a smile as wide as the horizon over water. And as much as I wish it, I doubt she's in such a good mood over me."

Jacob turned around, nearly forgetting his friend was standing beside him. His brain only seemed to recognize the beautiful, golden-brown woman with that luscious body that tied him in knots and then some. She walked toward him with the enticing rhythm of her swaying hips pulling him further under her spell.

"Don't let *dinner* keep you up all night, my friend. The Slick Six needs you functioning on all cylinders to make this visit work."

Jacob knew Matt was speaking the truth. But somehow as Keely stepped closer to him, the only thing he seemed to be able to focus on was her.

He'd debate with himself later about how problematic his thoughts were. But right now, the only thing he wanted was to walk back to his house so he could spend as much time as he could revisiting all the wonderful things about Keely and her body that he just couldn't manage to get enough of.

Why does that man look this good in dusty jeans and a faded plaid shirt? There has to be a law.

If there wasn't, there sure as hell should be. No one, absolutely no one, had the right to be that sexy standing in dirt and grass and all other manner of nature that her city-girl self was usually so far removed from. Concrete was her happy place and greenery usually made her nervous. But everything about the Slick Six ranch made her feel like dirt and the smell of trees and hay were her new oasis. That was all for one reason only. Jacob Chatman.

Jacob Chatman was somehow changing her slowly but surely, and as much as she wanted to pretend it was nothing, it was definitely something.

And if she doubted that, one look at him standing on his ranch, looking like the poster boy for sexy and rugged cowboys everywhere, and she forgot how to focus on anything but him.

The fact that she was out here instead of being hunched over her iPad jotting down notes or stitching the million and one buttons onto Ariana's dress was proof that she only had Jacob on the brain.

"Howdy, Ms. Tucker."

Keely heard Matt's voice, but she didn't bother to take her eyes off Jacob. As fine as he was, she was certain Matt could forgive her this momentary lack in social graces.

"Hey, Matt." Her voice was bright, and her step had just a bit more pep in it as she stopped in front of Jacob. Matt chuckled, his voice getting more and more distant, signaling the fact that he was moving away from them.

"Well, I'll leave you to it, Ms. Tucker. I can see already that you're the cure for Jacob's sourpuss mood."

Matt's parting words barely registered through the haze being around Jacob caused. Without thinking about where they were or who was around them, she raised her arms and hooked them around Jacob's neck.

It took only a split second to realize how forward she was being. She and Jacob had never talked about public displays of affection before. He was at work, even if he owned the place. Maybe this wasn't such a good look.

He must've sensed her hesitation, because just as she was preparing to step back, Jacob wrapped his arm around her and pulled her closer to him.

"You don't ever have to question me wanting your hands on me."

"Thank you for that." She linked her arms around his neck again. "But I should've asked before I just assumed. Now—" she sought his gaze, needing to connect with him "—what was Matt saying about your mood?"

She could feel the muscles in his shoulders and neck tense. Instinctively, she began kneading the strong line of his neck with her fingers, hoping to relax him.

"Is everything okay?"

"Yes and no," he replied, huffing an exhausted breath into the air. "I'm just anxious about this visit. There's so much riding on it that it's got my back up. I'm not proud of the fact that I took it out on Matt."

Keely felt for him. She understood this kind of anxiety and the pressure owning a business put you under. When it was your company, everything began and ended with you.

"Anything I can do to help?"

"There is, but we should probably take it indoors."

She shook her head. Even under the pressure of anxiety, he still seemed to remember how well their bodies fit together when they were naked.

"It's cute how you really thought it would be that easy to get me into bed."

"Come on, Keely," he whispered in her ear. "Help a brotha out."

With his Texas twang, that phrase was slightly comical coming from him. Aside from how good the sex was, it was moments like these where they let themselves be the slightest bit silly with one another that was creating a bond between them. She'd been here for nearly two weeks, and she felt so comfortable in his presence that it should worry her.

It didn't.

It should. But being with him felt so good that she'd resigned herself to the ache she knew she would feel when she finally had to go back to her real life and leave Royal.

Keely wasn't a masochist. She didn't seek out pain. She was falling for Jacob Chatman and she liked it. Even though she knew that ultimately this thing that was building between them had an expiration date on it.

"We can have a good time tonight when we're both finished with work. But if there's anything else I can do to help between now and then, I'd be glad to lend a hand."

He lifted his brow, searching her gaze before he spoke again.

"Do you mean that?"

"Of course I do. What do you need?"

Jacob looked up to the open sky, taking it in as if he needed strength to continue. When his gaze met hers again, she could see his earlier anxiety returning.

"Me talking about the ranch and what we offer on the grounds is easy for me. My work is there to speak for me. But people like Ezra Stanley require schmoozing, and I'm not really the best at that. That's where I need you to come in."

"How so?"

"I have to take him to the Texas Cattleman's Club to wine and dine him after the tour. The idea of small talk and me saying something foolish is going to worry a hole in my gut. So, I was hoping you'd attend the dinner with me to keep me from shoving my foot in my mouth."

She stepped back, running her fingers through her hair with one hand as she pulled out her phone and scrolled through her calendar with the other. She didn't need to look at the schedule to already know she had a conflict. But when she looked up at him and saw the silent "pretty please" in his eyes, she knew she had to finagle some things to make this a possibility.

"I'm supposed to be meeting with the florist during that time."

She could tell by the sad, puppy dog eyes he was giving her that he was anticipating her no. That certainly should've been her answer considering how important this meeting was to both finishing Ariana's dress and coordinating its accents into the wedding and reception.

"It's all right, Keely. I would never ask you to compromise your work for mine."

She smiled at him then, genuinely relieved at his statement.

"Thank you for respecting my work as much as yours." She took a deep breath and did some mental maneuvering to see if there was any way she could move some things around.

"Let me call the vendor and see if she'll be agreeable to seeing me a bit earlier. I hate to make last-minute changes, but this is important, you're important."

It wasn't the yes he wanted but she could tell he was grateful for the maybe she was offering instead. And knowing she put that glowing spark of hope in his eyes made her happier than a trip to the fabric store.

Keely, girl. What is you doing?

Seventeen

"Welcome to Sheen. How may I help you?"

Keely's gaze followed the voice offering her the warm greeting until her eyes found a very tall man with straight ink-black hair and a light beard staring back at her. At five feet ten inches, Keely didn't often find men so much taller than her that she'd classify them as tall. This man, however, had to stand at least five to seven inches above her head.

"Hi, I'm Keely Tucker of Low-Kee Designs. I'm here to meet with Corryna Lawson."

Bright blue eyes flashed at her as he extended his hand.

"You're in luck, she's already here waiting for you."

Keely eagerly followed him to the back, stealing a quick glance around the dimly lit restaurant as she went.

"Ms. Tucker," the host began, "this is Ms. Lawson." He looked down at Corryna before speaking again. "Ms. Lawson, this is Ms. Tucker of Low-Kee Designs."

With a nod from both women, the host made his exit. Keely shook Corryna's hand before sitting and quickly pulled out her trusty iPad mini to start taking notes. As soon as she pulled her Apple Pencil from its case, she noted the time. She didn't have a moment to lose if she was going to glam up to sit by Jacob's side tonight.

"Well, there is one thing I need from you to make our bride a happy camper." Corryna stared at Keely with wide green eyes, waiting in anticipation for her to drop the proverbial other shoe. "I'm gonna need a ridiculous amount of bluebonnet flowers. I'm talking enough for bouquets and boutonnieres, ceremony decorations and table centerpieces at the reception hall. Essentially, I need to know if you can you make it rain bluebonnets. Can you do that?"

A slow smile beamed on Corryna's face before she answered, "Hell yeah."

"Keely, we're gonna be late."

Jacob paced back and forth in the kitchen as nervous energy coursed through him as he watched each moment on the wall clock ticking by. He'd been up before the sun to make certain everything was perfect for Ezra Stanley's visit. Jacob had personally escorted the man every place his feet had touched on Chatman land.

Ezra was a squat man with blond hair and dark brown eyes who wore big shades and an even bigger hat. But whatever he lacked in height, he more than made up for in his knowledge of and love for horses. He'd pressed Jacob about his methods, his philosophies and outcomes when it came to horse training. He'd taken such careful inspection of the premises, Jacob was certain he was more thorough than any state inspector that had ever come through the Slick Six.

No matter how vigorous the interview process had been, Jacob had come away from the experience confident that he was more than halfway to securing what would be a very lucrative contract. All that remained was this dinner, and if Jacob understood, it wasn't about mingling, it was to look Jacob in his eye and see if he could be trusted with such a precious gift as his horse.

If he was handing Tildy over to a stranger, he'd want to know if the man could be trusted to take care of his dear companion too.

"Keely!" he hollered again, rubbing the back of his neck as he tried to calm himself down. Getting tense this close to his dinner meeting wouldn't do him any favors.

"Jacob, stop screaming the walls down. Creating this kind of perfection takes time."

He turned around with a sly barb on the tip of his

tongue, but the smart-ass comment dried up when his gaze took her in.

Their dinner wasn't formal, but the Texas Cattleman's Club was upscale enough that even he dug a suit out of his closet and threw it on. Keely wore a white bodycon dress that made her look like sin and heaven all rolled up into one.

"I rest my case." He couldn't get upset at her remark, or the fact that she'd taken so long to get ready. Watching her strut past him with an extra sway in her hips as she glided on those impossibly high heels she was wearing, he realized two things. First, she knew she was the total package. Two, she also knew that he knew she was the total package.

He shook his head, trying to get his wayward mind to focus. "Keely, the point of you attending this dinner is to calm me down, not raise my blood pressure."

She turned slowly, waiting for him to catch up to her. She cupped his cheek, giving him a playful wink as their eyes met.

"The point of me attending this dinner is to keep your anxiety-fueled bad mood in check while you try to schmooze Stanley. So, tell me, are you thinking about your anxiety right now?"

He sure as shit wasn't, not by a long shot.

When she knew she'd made her point, she turned toward the door again. "Come along, Jacob. I wouldn't want you to be late."

Late? He couldn't give a damn about late right now. All he wanted was to continue to watch her strut back and forth in his kitchen as if she were on a runway. To follow behind her until he was close enough to wrap his arms around her and pull her flush against him. But duty did call. So, he vowed he'd do his level best at this dinner to keep things running smoothly, because outside of this contract, there was nothing as important to him as peeling that dress off Keely the moment they stepped through his front door.

He watched her saunter out onto the front porch, the sway of her hips nearly lulling him into a trance. He lifted his eyes to the night sky and shook his head.

"If anyone is up there listening, help me keep my eyes off this woman long enough to get us there and back safely."

He opened the passenger door and saw her safely seated before he slipped inside of his driver's seat. When he did, he found her shifting items in the small clutch purse on her lap.

"You forget something?"

She looked up, her body relaxing as she closed the purse and settled into her seat. "No." She pulled the key to the great room out of the purse for him to get a quick glimpse of it before she tucked it away. "I changed so fast, I just needed to double-check that I had this key on me. I didn't have a chance to do my usual check when I'm moving things from one bag to the other."

He kept his eyes on the road, but lifted a sharp brow. "*Fast* is relative."

She squeezed his thigh playfully. "Whatever. I told

you that this level of perfection takes time to achieve. I essentially performed a miracle in less than an hour."

"You're actually carrying that thing around. You could've left it in the bedroom."

She shook her head. "Not on your life," she replied. "This key never leaves my possession. As long as Ariana's dress is in there, no one can go in or out of that room except me."

"Is there really this much interest in what Ariana is wearing on her wedding day? I get that she's a celebrity, but most folks around here don't care about her or Xavier's notoriety. We treat 'em like normal folks."

"This town is built different, I guess. Ariana can barely eat without someone snapping photos of her." She looked out the window, watching the road pass by as if she needed time to contemplate what she was about to say next. "Not to mention, there's this celebrity wedding crasher that has Ariana and Ex's wedding on his radar. If he got hold of any information, he'd leak it all over his social media just for clicks. It would devastate Ariana and ruin my business. No celebrity would ever trust me to work on another design."

He could feel tension building in her through the hand she still had propped on his leg.

"I know to most people, what I do doesn't seem all that important. But this is my passion and I take it seriously."

There was something about the dip in her voice

that conveyed how serious she was. As if she'd had to have this conversation one too many times in her past.

The idea that she'd been forced to justify herself, her choices, didn't sit well with him. His arms twitched with the need to scoop her out of her seat and pull her as close to him as she could get.

Since being confined in a car made that sort of impossible, he slid his right hand over hers, lacing his fingers through hers, pulling her hand to his lips and placing a comforting kiss there.

"There is nothing frivolous about what you do. If I gave you the impression that's how I felt, I don't. I see how damn hard you work. It's evident in the details of your creations."

He could see her shift in her seat from his periphery.

"You've seen my work?"

The surprise in her voice tickled him. It was an addictive sound, sparking something bright inside him that he wanted to stick around. Not because it felt good to him, but because he enjoyed knowing he could give her something no one else could.

"Of course I have. After watching how dedicated you are to creating the perfect dress for Ariana, there's no way I wouldn't want to see more of your work. I may have even purchased an item or two from your men's business collection."

She turned in her seat, with an amused but confused smile blooming on her lips.

"I'm trying to figure out where a cowboy who

loves denim like a mouse loves cheese is gonna wear one of my designs."

He shrugged. "On occasions like tonight where I'm forced to leave the land and play in society. Also, I figured it would make a good impression on you if I showed up in New York to take you out on a proper date."

When she didn't immediately respond, he wondered if he was presuming too much. Keely had never made mention of wanting to see him outside of her time in Royal. He fought the desire to squirm. Instead, he straightened his spine as best he could in his seat.

"That is…if you'd care to keep seeing me when you go back home."

Before she could answer, the Texas Cattleman's Club came into view and he could see Ezra getting out of his car ahead of them in the valet line. Now, instead of worrying about how this dinner was going to go with Ezra, it seemed he'd spend his time worrying about Keely's answer.

"I tell you, I've been to some of the finest restaurants in the world, and there is no one on this planet that knows how to cook a steak like Texans."

Keely watched Ezra stab the last piece of steak on his plate and couldn't fight the enjoyment that stirred in her while taking in his antics. She hadn't known exactly what to expect of him. While he was inspecting the ranch and interviewing Jacob and his team, Keely had been tweaking her sketches and sewing her behind off to make up for the time she knew she would miss while acting as Jacob's wingman. As tense as Jacob had been about this meeting, she'd expected an uptight asshole.

"No offense to your home state, Ms. Keely." He popped the perfectly cooked piece of meat in his mouth and hummed in satisfaction. "But even New York steakhouses don't have a thing on this."

"I'm not offended." Keely picked up her fork to finish off her own steak. "The truth is the truth. This is one helluva good piece of meat." She cut her eyes at Jacob, thoroughly entertained by his attempt to keep from choking on the broccoli he was currently chewing.

"Smart, beautiful, honest and eats more than twigs in front of people. Where on earth did you ever find someone like her, Jacob?" Before Jacob could answer, Ezra turned to Keely and gave her a genuine smile. In Keely's industry, she'd come across enough men who wore their sleaze like a bad cologne. This wasn't some lecherous old man. This was charm gained through experience with a little flirting to boot. "Do you have a sister?"

"I do," Keely answered. "But she's taken too."

She'd picked up her wineglass and had it less than an inch from her mouth when she realized what she'd said. She chanced a glimpse at Jacob to see if he'd heard her slipup. The moment their gazes collided, she knew he heard exactly what she'd said.

If the sharp look in his eye didn't clue her in, then the way his jaw tightened certainly did. The only problem was she didn't know if his reaction was good or bad.

Tiny spikes of cold sliced through her as she waited for this awkward impasse they were having while sitting at a table in the fanciest place in Royal, Texas.

"I didn't find her. She found me." Jacob may have been answering Ezra's question, but the way he looked at her, with so much heat in his eyes, she could feel her skin being singed by the flames. "And every day since, I wake up asking what I did to get so lucky."

The world narrowed down to the two of them. The voices of their fellow diners became insignificant murmurs. The large dining room became a tight corner with only room for the two of them, and the air was so thin, she felt light-headed from the lack of oxygen.

Her fingers began to tingle and somehow, without her recognizing how, her glass went from sitting firmly in her hand to lying on its side on the table. The heavy thud of the crystal against the cloth-covered table snapped her out of whatever strange trance Jacob's voice had lulled her into.

And when he opened his mouth to speak, she interrupted.

"My goodness," she exclaimed. "Seems that all that time sewing yesterday has given me a case of butterfingers." She grabbed her napkin and dabbed up some of the excess liquid spreading on the thick table linen, getting her hands sticky with it. "Excuse me, gentlemen, I'm gonna find my way to the restroom and wash my hands."

She stood up and let her stilettos carry her as quickly as they could from Jacob's scrutiny. Because whatever that was that happened between them sure as hell wasn't the fun they'd both signed on for. This… This was as serious as serious could get.

Eighteen

"Who are you?"

Keely sat at one of the stools along the vanity that took up one wall of the anteroom in the TCC's ladies' room.

She was fortunate enough that room had been empty when she'd entered in a near state of panic. As relieved as she was to find a precious few moments alone, she knew at some point, someone would find their way inside her hiding space, and unless she wanted them to see her falling apart, she'd have to get herself together.

Keely didn't have to ask herself why she was so out of sorts. That answer was clear. Jacob Chatman had made her feel easy enough around him that she'd let some Freudian-type slipup reveal something she hadn't even admitted to herself. She wanted Jacob Chatman. All of him. Not just the great-sex part, or the "he's funny and makes me laugh" parts. She wanted every piece that made up the sexy cowboy. She didn't just want him, she wanted to tattoo "Property of Keely Tucker" across his forehead so everyone would know, including him, that he belonged to her.

She released a deep breath and let that admission settle into her bones, seeping down into the marrow of her being. She wanted Jacob Chatman. But more importantly, she wanted to belong to Jacob Chatman too, and that reality would bring so much chaos into her life, she knew it was something she should never have.

She was here for work. Yeah, she'd taken the meetings she'd needed to. But she hadn't put in half the stitchwork that she should have by now. She was supposed to leave next week. The gown's first iteration should've been done by then.

If she were home in her little studio, nothing could've taken her focus away. But languishing on his ranch and in his arms, Keely had pushed her work to the side, not because Jacob had asked her to, but because everything in her being wanted to focus on him and the pleasure she derived from being with him, rather than do her work.

She couldn't blame this on Jacob. He wasn't some chauvinist demanding she give him all her time and attention. He never acted as if her work wasn't as important as his. This was all Keely. That meant only she could take responsibility for it. She had to fix this somehow. She had to extricate herself from the pull Jacob had on her. Otherwise, when this was over, her career would be in tatters, and she'd have no one to blame but herself.

Committed to holding herself accountable, she opened her clutch, rooting around in it for her lipstick. Feeling more confident once she'd applied the rich color, she smiled at herself.

"You can do this, Keely. It's about your work. You've made a million sacrifices to get this far, this is just one more."

Satisfied with her pep talk, she dropped the lipstick back in her purse and rooted around to take a glimpse of the great room key. Concern nipped at the edges of the encouragement she'd just given herself when she couldn't find it.

On the verge of a panic attack, she dumped everything out of the small purse onto the vanity table, hoping to find the key underneath her compact. But she knew her luck wasn't that good. Somehow, between getting out of Jacob's car and entering the TCC, she'd lost the literal key to her success all because she'd put her focus on the wrong thing: Jacob.

"You are one lucky bastard."

Jacob pulled his eyes away from Keely's disappearing form to focus on Ezra. The task was more difficult than it should have been, because his head was so preoccupied with whatever had just happened between Keely and him before she bolted for the bathroom.

"Trust me, I know." Jacob saw no need to sugarcoat his response or pretend he didn't know what Ezra was talking about. He didn't want to pretend where Keely was concerned.

He picked up his glass at that realization, needing to wet his suddenly dry mouth. Keely was a beautiful woman and any man would be lucky to have her. The fact that she'd chosen to spend her precious time with him made him feel as if there was no man in the world that could compete with him, not when he held the interest of the best woman who was the best at everything.

He lightly shook his head as a small, amused smile bent the corner of his mouth. This woman had gotten under his skin and that fact should make him anxious, scared; he should be planning a tactical retreat. Instead, he wanted to run to Keely, to announce it to everyone who would listen that he was the most fortunate man alive.

"I like that."

Jacob raised a questioning brow, trying to figure out if he'd missed out on part of Ezra's conversation while his mind was focused on Keely.

"Like what?"

"The fact that you're smitten with Ms. Tucker and you don't have even the slightest inclination to hide it. I like that you recognize you have a gem in that lovely young woman who graced us with her presence tonight. Everything about the way you are with her shows me you have the kindness and the resilience to care for my horse."

"You're basing your decision to give me your business on my choice in a woman?"

Jacob was hoping this wasn't a blatant display of chauvinism. So far, everything the man had said about Keely had been complimentary. Jacob wasn't certain if that remained to be the case so he waited, leaving the pause after his question to convey his need for Ezra to expand on his statement.

"I'm not that foolish or sentimental. Your facility is top-notch and your training techniques are some of the most innovative I've ever seen. Not to mention, your outcomes are nothing to dismiss either. You know what the hell you're doing when it comes to horses. But I could find a hundred horse trainers who could do the same. There has to be something more."

Jacob tilted his head, still not completely understanding where Ezra was going with this conversation.

"And you think Keely is that something more?"

Ezra leaned forward, bracing his forearms on the table. "Your companion is a powerful woman who is entirely her own being. Some men would be foolish enough to try to smother the light that exudes from her. But you're wise enough to understand that controlling beauty and power is much less rewarding than giving it the room to grow and thrive. If you can understand that with a force like your Ms. Tucker, then you'll certainly do fine with my horse, who is equally as aware of her power as Ms. Tucker is. So, if you want my business, the contract is yours."

Ezra stood, extending his hand to Jacob, who gladly accepted the gesture.

"I'm gonna head on out. Please share my goodbyes with Ms. Tucker. I'll have my lawyers contact you tomorrow about the contract. I look forward to working with you."

Ezra gave Jacob's hand an excited squeeze before he headed toward the door, leaving Jacob to contemplate all the man had said.

Of all the things Jacob had expected to hear from Ezra, an endorsement of his connection to Keely hadn't been it. Not by a long shot. But as Jacob took in the man's words and settled into his seat, he knew Ezra wasn't wrong. Ezra's observation had one other purpose. It sparked this burning need to lock things down where Keely was concerned.

He wanted more than just fun in and out of bed. And as he looked in the direction Keely had walked, he knew it was high time he shared those desires with Keely. If he was as lucky as Ezra believed, then maybe she'd have him as something more than a friend with benefits. Because the more time he spent with Keely, the more he realized she wasn't just a friend. With her fun and flirty ways, her supportive nature and her singular focus on her own excellence, Keely was fast becoming the woman of his dreams. Now, he just had to convince her of that fact.

But when he turned his head in the direction of the restrooms to see Keely walking quickly toward the table with sharp lines drawn on her face, he pushed his ruminating thoughts aside to focus on what looked like panic settling across Keely's face.

He stood before she reached the table, placing a calm hand against her cheek as soon as he met her.

"What's wrong?"

"It's the key, Jacob. I've lost the key."

Fear gripped him, squeezing tightly around his rib cage as he processed what she'd just said and what it meant. Nodding, he grabbed her hand, and headed back to their table. He released her hand long enough to wave and catch their server's attention.

"Put all of this on my tab and give yourself a healthy tip."

Before the server could nod in agreement, Jacob grabbed Keely's hand, directing her to the exit.

With each step, his heart rate ticked up another anxious notch, mostly because he could feel her worry turning into tense panic as each moment passed. But there was also another reason, a wholly selfish reason, he easily admitted to himself. If they didn't find this damn key, his plans of talking to Keely about their situation-ship were as good as dead in the water.

Jacob pulled his car into the garage. He'd usually let it sit in the driveway, but he needed the light the structure could offer. He spared a quick glance to find Keely sitting ramrod straight, her body practically vibrating with tension.

He shut off the car, and when she reached for her door, he rested his hand on her thigh and gave it a gentle squeeze. The touch wasn't meant to be sensual. It was all about comfort, about unraveling the knot he'd watched her twist herself into the moment she told him she'd lost the key.

He'd done his best to look around in the car once they left the TCC. But with the pitch-black dark surrounding them, and few streetlights, even with the flashlights from their phones and the small flashlight he kept in his glove compartment, there was no way they could sweep through the car the way they needed to.

"We'll find it, Keely. The last place you had it was in the car. It probably slipped out of your purse when you rested it on your seat."

She shared a soft smile with him, one he assumed was for his benefit, not hers. However, he'd spent enough time staring into her eyes that he could see they were still fraught with worry.

"Go on up and change and we'll start looking when you get back."

She nodded, silently exiting the car. Jacob stepped out of the car, pulling off his jacket and heading straight for the tools lined up against the garage walls. He grabbed his father's old-school droplight, plugging it up quickly before kneeling down on the concrete floor to inspect the passenger seat.

He was sure his suit pants would be ruined by the time this was over. It was a small price to pay for Keely's peace of mind, as far as he was concerned.

He looked in every crevice in the passenger seat, the floor, between the cushions, the well in the door. It wasn't until he opened the back door and looked behind Keely's seat that he saw something sparkle when the light touched it. It was wedged between the seat and the wall of the car. There was no way his big fingers were fitting in that space. He moved back to the wall to get a flathead screwdriver. Within seconds, he'd pushed the metal object to the floor of the back seat.

He huffed a sigh of relief when he picked it up, confirming it was the key. If they hadn't found it, he would've just changed the locks to give her secure access again. But that would've had to wait until he could get a new lock from the hardware store in the morning. The idea of her spending the entire night tied up in worry and fear was something he couldn't tolerate, so here he was, on his knees in one of the few pairs of good pants he had, fiddling with a drop-light and a screwdriver.

Keely's return to the garage brought a smile to his face, and when he stood up, waving the key in the air for her to see, the relief spreading throughout her entire body was well worth the effort.

"Thank goodness! Where did you find it?"

"Wedged between your seat and the side panel. I told you it was just too dark for us to see properly at the club."

He stepped closer to her, placing the key in her hand and noting how tightly she clutched the piece of metal. Despite holding the key in her hand, her eyes were still serious, and her mouth was pulled taught into a flat line, making him wonder if this was just her way of processing her earlier fear, or if this was something else.

He placed a gentle kiss on her lips and felt no response to it. He pulled back, his gaze searching hers, but her stare was nearly blank.

"Hey, it's been a day and you've had a lot of excitement at the end of it. Why don't you let me draw you a bath or give you a massage to help you relax?"

She stepped back from him, putting what he could see was intentional distance between them.

"Thanks for the offer. As tempting as it is, I'm gonna have to ask for a rain check. I need to get in some stitchwork tonight."

"At this hour?"

"We're business owners. You know we don't punch a clock."

She turned to the door that connected the garage to the house. Just before stepping through, she looked over her shoulder at him.

"I know you need to get up early. Don't wait up. I'll be up as soon as I can."

She gave him a final nod as the definitive end to their conversation. As he stood there alone in the quiet garage, he couldn't help but feel that gesture foretold something ominous he wasn't going to like one bit.

Nineteen

Keely bent down to spread the train of the dress out as she prepped for her video chat with Ariana to show her the new elements she'd added to the dress.

Her neck and back cracked when she tried to stand upright, a clear indicator that sleeping on a couch for days at a time to avoid the man sleeping in a bed above her wasn't the smartest idea.

She rolled her neck, trying to distract herself from the conflicting thoughts bouncing around in her head. She was almost there, almost to a place where her professional mask could push down the big emotions threatening to swallow her whole, when a knock at the door broke through her concentration.

"Keely?"

She didn't need to open the door to see who was on

the other side. She knew that deep voice that coiled around her like a thick python, squeezing out every bit of resistance she attempted to muster up.

It is his house, Keely. It's not like you can refuse him entry.

Yes, it was his home. But she also knew Jacob well enough that he would not tread where he wasn't welcome. Before she could continue that line of thinking, another knock landed hard on the door, making her reconsider her thoughts of the limits of Jacob's actions. The booming sound was loud enough, she figured if she made him wait any longer, he might do something drastic like take the door off the hinges to see why she wasn't responding.

"Be right there."

She opened the door, and there he stood in his usual work uniform, a plaid shirt that stretched across his torso in an almost obscene fashion. As he walked by her, settling into the great room, she realized his jeans were presenting an equally tempting picture of the lower half of his body.

Keep your head together, girl. Your work is all that matters.

Keely took a breath as she closed the door, repeating that mantra over and over again in hopes that it would give her the fortitude to do what she needed to do: keep her head and her heart focused on leveling up her business and ignoring anything else that didn't fall in line with that.

"Did you need something?"

His eyes contracted into tiny slits, his gaze sweeping over her like searchlights looking for the guilty.

"Look," he began cautiously. "I don't mean to upset you, but I feel like something's changed between us and not in a good way."

She walked over to the mannequin in the center of the room, fiddling with the stitching on a side panel. There was nothing wrong with it. It was perfect, nothing less than Keely's usual when she was in her zone. But that was the problem. She hadn't been in that zone since she'd met Jacob.

"I'm not sure I know what you're talking about."

She spared him long enough of a glance that she could see the muscle at the side of his jaw twitch in frustration.

"I'm talking about the fact that I haven't seen you in days. It's beginning to feel like you're avoiding me."

No one could ever accuse that man of being stupid. Without much difficulty, he'd figured out her ruse. But just because he'd figured her out didn't mean she had to admit that he was right. Denial was the name of this game, and she'd hold on to it for as long as she could.

"Listen." She tried her best to sound annoyed, trying to forget the way his smoldering gaze made her burn for him, trying to keep the need out of her voice. "I'm not sure what you think is going on, but I'm working. We both know that's what I came here for so I'm not exactly certain why you're trippin'."

His nares widened as he drew in a deep breath, placing his hands on his waist.

"Why I'm trippin'?" She could see the anger building in his stiff stance and tight features. But underneath the frustration, she also saw a glimpse of something like disappointment coloring his dark irises. "I know what you're doing, Keely. It doesn't have to be this way."

She turned away from him, locking her joints, forcing her posture to be ramrod straight. She knew if she saw the same need in his eyes that she was certain filled her own, she'd never be able to resist him.

"This cowardly bullshit is beneath you, Keely. I thought you had more heart than this."

So did she, but apparently her feelings for him had changed her on a chemical level. She was changed. And as she listened to him walk out of the great room, the quiet click of the closing door resonating like a loud gong, vibrating off the walls, she wondered if she would ever be the same again.

For fifteen minutes she stood in the room, praying Jacob would return while simultaneously hoping that he'd be strong enough for the both of them and keep his distance. Her chest felt heavy as if some kind of heft pressed down against it, restricting her breathing.

She wanted to curl up and bawl her eyes out, but duty called. Her meeting with Ariana was moments away, and she had to prepare herself.

She gripped the back of a nearby high-back chair,

squeezing until her fingers ached and her palms blanched from the pressure.

She knew she didn't have to punish herself like this. But the pain of the carved wood biting into her skin was much more preferable than feeling that gaping chasm that was growing between them.

But as her mind lingered on his parting words, she realized she was punishing Jacob for a crime he hadn't committed. He hadn't done anything wrong, and her needing distance wasn't about him. It was about her needing to focus. Yet she couldn't bring herself to tell him those words. Not when there was so much riding on her ability to stay away from him.

She stayed downstairs stitching or sketching away until she was too exhausted to climb the stairs, settling for the couch, using his early sleep schedule as a means to put distance between them.

Trifling. Just trifling.

She would've agreed with herself except her FaceTime notification on her iPad mini broke through her thoughts, giving her a momentary reprieve from her mixed emotions.

"Hey, Ariana."

"Hey, girl," Ariana replied as her huge smile filled the screen. "How's my dress coming along?"

"I won't lie, even though I suggested them, it took me a bit to figure out how to get the bluebonnet accents into the dress. But I think I've got it now. You ready?"

Ariana squealed at the sight of her dress and it

made all the discomfort Keely was experiencing before the call slowly abate.

"Keely, I know it's essentially just the frame without all the adornments and embroidery, but this is magnificent. I can't wait to try it on. You were right, the bluebonnet accents were the perfect addition."

Keely's neck began to ache again and she couldn't help rubbing it in front of the camera.

"You okay?"

It was a simple question, but Keely wasn't sure how to answer Ariana. Sure, save for the few kinks she'd developed from sleeping on the couch, she was physically fine. But how did she explain this hefty weight sitting on her chest that grew larger and more powerful every minute she kept herself away from Jacob?

"I'm fine. My neck's just a little out of whack from working too long without enough breaks."

"Well," Ariana said with a sparkle of something wicked in her eyes. "We absolutely can't have that. When I hang up this phone, I'm gonna book you into a spa for a full day of pampering."

"You don't have to do that, Ariana. You're paying me a ridiculous amount of money for this dress. That's compensation enough."

Ariana shook her head like a displeased schoolteacher. "I'll hear nothing of it."

Keely attempted to open her mouth in protest, but Ariana held up a silencing finger, relaying her position on the matter was final.

"All right, I'll accept your generous offer. Besides,

afterward, maybe I can hook up with my girlfriend Zanai and her best friend, Morgan, so I can catch up with Zanai and discuss some final thoughts on the fabric selections for the bridesmaids' dresses with Morgan too."

"I have a better suggestion. Find out Zanai's and Morgan's availability and I'll send all three of you."

Before Keely could protest, Ariana waved her hand as she smiled. "Send me the deets and I'll set it up. Later."

And just like that, Ariana was gone.

"No wonder she's such a great producer and actress. She has no problems getting exactly what she wants."

Figuring it was easier to go along instead of argue at this point, Keely found her phone on a nearby end table and called Zanai. Maybe hanging out with her old friend would help her clear some of the fog in her head. Because one way or the other, Keely had to get her head right.

Keely moaned as the loose feeling permeating every muscle, tendon and bone she possessed moved through her body.

She managed to find just enough energy to turn her head to find her two companions in much the same condition. Zanai was stretched out on her back, and Morgan was on her side gently cradling her baby bump.

Keely lay on her stomach with her arms crossed underneath the plush pillow cradling her head.

"This is the life," Zanai half whispered in response to Keely's satisfied moan.

"You mean rich folks don't indulge in spa treatments like this every other day and twice on Sunday?"

Morgan lifted her sleep mask from her eyes and peeked over at Zanai, then they both turned their gazes to Keely and answered, "Hell no," simultaneously.

"We're too busy working ourselves to the bone." Morgan's comment brought an amused smile to Zanai's face. "Since I cut ties with my dad, I'm a broke health care worker. There's no way I could afford to splurge like this on the regular. Please send my thanks to Ariana."

Morgan threw a small hand towel at Zanai that landed on her leg.

"Yeah," Morgan countered, "but she's got a rich boyfriend who would love to pamper her like this if she'd allow it."

Keely turned onto her side to get a better look at Zanai. "Girl, what is wrong with you. You'd better let that man spoil you."

"Trust me." Morgan's voice pulled their attention. "I am wholeheartedly supporting Ryan's spoiling of me while I'm carrying his child."

"Lucky heifers," Keely groused, drawing the collective laughter of the two women.

"I can't believe a woman as gorgeous and successful as you doesn't have her pick of suitors. If you wanted someone, all you'd have to do is bat your beautiful lashes. Those Hollywood folks have to be blind."

If only Morgan's assumption was correct. Keely was in celebrity circles all the time. But it was work. And since she didn't play where she ate, all of these beautiful suitors Morgan was mentioning were non-existent.

"First, I don't live in Hollywood. I'm in New York. But even if I were, I'm just too busy to focus on a relationship."

Zanai lifted her brow, silently noting Keely's BS the way only a longtime friend could.

"So, you're saying there's no one tickling your fancy?" Zanai countered.

The lie was on the tip of her tongue, but when Morgan's and Zanai's dual gazes locked on her, she realized she just didn't have the energy for pretense. She sat up on her table, preparing to bare her soul. Maybe talking it out would help her work through the conflict in her head.

"Whatever I tell you two has to stay between us." They both eagerly nodded, sitting up on their individual massage tables, giving her their rapt attention.

"Jacob Chatman and I have been indulging in a lighthearted fling for the last two weeks and everything about it has been wonderful."

Her shoulders dropped with the last syllable spoken and the two women with her leaned in with concern painted across their faces.

"You sound like that's a bad thing."

"It is, Morgan," Keely replied on an exhausted huff.

"But why?" Zanai's question was logical. Unfortunately, logic had nothing to do with how Jacob made Keely feel.

"He's a distraction from my work. A very sexy distraction, granted. But still, a distraction. Every time he touches me, every time he slides me that slick look of his, every time he winks and crooks his finger, and uses that deep Texas drawl of his to say 'Come here, thickness,' it's all too damn distracting."

Morgan pointed a single finger up. "Wait a minute. Did you just say you find him calling you 'thickness' sexy, as in you like it?"

Keely smiled. As a size 16 woman and after spending so much time working in the rag industry, she understood Morgan's dismay. American beauty standards told women you have to be a size zero to be considered attractive and if you weren't, you should be ashamed of your body. Fortunately for Keely, she'd never subscribed to that limiting belief.

"I think it's more of a cultural thing, and beyond that, an individual situation. But culturally, Black people celebrate having larger bodies. So, when we say thick or thicc, we are actually using the word as a compliment, not a pejorative."

Zanai nodded in agreement with Keely. "She's right. If Jayden doesn't grab a handful of my ass every morning before I leave for work, I'm insulted and questioning if he's got a problem."

Keely couldn't help but chuckle at that. She couldn't

lie and say she didn't have an appreciation for a slap on the ass as a sign of appreciation between lovers. Some might find it crude, but to her, it tickled her fancy…a lot.

"I realize that people may have different experiences when it comes to body image and being called something like that can be triggering for them. But every time Jacob calls me 'thickness,' he's telling me how irresistibly sexy he finds me and how much he appreciates every roll and curve of my body. So yeah, it's kinda hot as hell and ultimately a distraction."

Morgan had a peculiar expression on her face and Keely wondered if she needed to clarify what she'd said any further.

"In that context, I can see how uplifting that is. But what I can't figure out is if you're enjoying him so much, why can't there be room for both work and Jacob in your life?"

"Because unlike you," Zanai began, "Keely doesn't understand how to balance being a business owner with having a life. It's the reason we haven't seen each other in so long."

Keely winced from the sting of Zanai's words. She could see by the concern and care in her friend's eyes that Zanai wasn't trying to be hurtful. But deep down, the truth of those words cut Keely deep.

Zanai gave Keely a compassionate smile, soothing over her singed feelings.

"I know it wasn't intentional, Keely. I'm so proud of what you've accomplished. But I'd be lying if I said

I didn't want you to make room for me, and people like Jacob, who from the sound of it, wants to care for you too."

"I wouldn't be so sure of that."

Morgan and Zanai shared a confused look before returning their questioning stares to Keely.

"Jacob is just as dedicated to his work as I am. He's not looking for anything deep. So, even if I were willing to try and make space for him, I'm not exactly sure he would want to pursue anything. We promised that we'd never interfere with each other's work. I can't just change the rules now."

Morgan slid down off her massage table, waddling carefully until she was standing next to Keely's table. "Sure, you can. Feelings change. And if the lovin' is as good as you seem to believe it is, isn't that worth the risk to everything else?"

"In a fantasy world, I'd say yes." Keely tapped her fingers on her table, the feedback helping her focus a bit on what was important. "But this is reality. And in my reality, if I'm distracted from work, I can't build the empire I'm striving for. I've put everything I have into this business. I can't just let it all go up in flames because Jacob Chatman is the sexiest thing walking."

Zanai cleared her throat to grab Keely's attention. "Let me put on my therapist's hat for a moment. Now granted, I don't practice general therapy, but I remember enough from my clinical rotations to give you a little bit of advice. Keely, I don't think your business is the problem at all. I think there's an even larger issue at play here."

Keely folded her arms like she used to when they were kids, bracing herself to hear something she knew she wasn't going to like.

"Okay, Dr. Z. Lay your rusty psychobabble on me."

Zanai laughed, keeping the levity in the room.

"I don't think Jacob being a distraction is the issue. The issue is, I think you've gone and fallen in love with Jacob Chatman and you're so determined to fight against it, you'll use any excuse to keep you from pursuing it."

Keely gripped the edge of her massage table to keep herself from falling over from that shot Zanai aimed at the center of her chest.

Panic grew inside her, but Keely had worked around too many celebrities not to have learned a trick or two about deflection. Because there was no way in hell she could explore this option, and all its complicated ramifications, while wrapped in a towel on a massage table with her friends.

"That's your theory, huh?" Keely quipped. "I'm afraid of being in love with Jacob? Well, if you're so smart, use your psychological superpowers to tell me why."

"That's something you've got to take the time and figure out on your own, Keely." Zanai left her table and walked over to Keely, placing a comforting hand on her shoulder. "And when you do, you need to talk to Jacob. There's no greater regret than the one of not trying at all."

Keely closed her eyes, pinching the bridge of her nose as she tried to keep it together. Zanai was right about one thing: Keely had some serious soul-searching to do. The question was, with less than a handful of days left in Royal, could she figure out what she wanted before it was too late?

Twenty

"I guess you're done avoiding me?"

The annoyance in Jacob's voice reached her long before she could see his sharp features as she walked into the stables.

"Jacob, I don't want to fight with you."

He stepped away from his horse to look at her, and the cold pouring off him made her shiver in the Texas heat.

"Seems of late you don't want to do much of anything with me, so I guess you're consistent at least."

"Jacob." She called his name again, hoping she could soothe his apparent irritation with her.

"What did I do?"

The sharp sound of his voice cut through the air. It was laced with anger, but she couldn't ignore the obvious pain mixed in it too.

"What do you mean?"

He placed both hands on his hips, staring her directly in the eye.

"Things were getting real good between you and me, Keely. I didn't imagine that. And then you just shut me out."

She shook her head, not because what he said wasn't true, but because it wasn't her intention to make him feel whatever he was feeling that had him so annoyed and angry with her.

"Don't deny it. You've been deliberately locking yourself away in that great room so you wouldn't have to be near me. And I need to know why. What did I do to screw things up so much that you don't even want to be in my presence? What were you punishing me for?"

The angry tick in his cheek compiled with the sadness clouding his eyes tugged at an invisible cord deep inside her. Unable to do anything to hold them back, she closed her eyes and let hot tears fall.

"You didn't do anything, Jacob. I wasn't trying to punish you." Her voice quavered and every bit of pride she had leaked out with her flowing tears. "I was trying to punish myself."

His world narrowed down to the wet streaks her falling tears left behind on her skin. Something possessive and raw clawed at him and the only thing his mind would let him entertain was pulling her into his arms and holding her until her quiet sobbing receded.

"I'm so sorry." Her face was pressed into his shoulder and her words were muffled, but he could still somehow make them out with perfect clarity. It was like everything else with Keely Tucker; he'd been hyperaware of her from the moment they met. That awareness had only become stronger, clearer as his feelings and desire for her had become less of a want and so much more than a need.

"I'm sorry too," he cooed while rubbing a flat palm against her back. "I shouldn't have attacked like that. I let my temper get the better of me and I should..."

She pulled away from him, seeking out his gaze and holding it firmly once her eyes found his.

"No, don't you dare apologize. You were right when you said this cowardly bullshit was beneath me. I should've come to you and talked to you. You deserve at least that much after the way I've treated you." She took another shaky breath, steadying herself by placing her palms flat against his chest.

He reveled in her closeness. The pressure of her body against his provided comfort the way nothing else had. But he knew he had to keep that to himself right now. Keely was as skittish as a new arrival on his ranch, and he'd bet money she would bolt if he didn't find a way to make her feel safe.

"Can we go back to the house and talk? Tildy and I are cool and all, but I don't need her up in my business right now."

The gentle-natured mare huffed, letting Keely know her comment wasn't appreciated. Tildy might be good-natured. But that didn't mean she still didn't have spunk.

Jacob cupped Keely's cheek, needing to hold their

connection. Things just made more sense when he was this close to her.

"I've got a better idea. You up for a ride?" He could see the protest building on her lips. The house was closer, but there was something magical about riding on his land, and right now, with them both wound so tightly, they needed some recreational activity to clear their heads. "We'll nix all this weirdness that's been going on for the last few days between us and hopefully, you'll find the words you're looking for."

With a nod, she acquiesced, and he took her hand, leading her to Tildy's stall.

"Now, I'm not trying to tell you what to do." He pointed his finger toward Tildy's bobbing head, smiling down at Keely. "But iffin' I was, I'd suggest you apologize to old Tildy before you saddle up. Nothing like a sore rump from a bad ride with a horse that's got you in her crosshairs."

They took a leisurely and silent ride to the outpost they'd settled in when they'd fixed the transformer. The last time they were here, they'd both let down their walls enough to find something exceptional between them. There was no doubt in his mind that if they could just get there, shut out the rest of the world, that maybe they could wade through the confusion they'd found themselves in.

They dismounted, and Jacob removed their tack as he prepared to send the horses off to frolic. He stopped, waiting for her to join him at his side, when he heard Keely speaking in a hushed voice to Tildy.

She'd been cautious but open with the horse since the first day he'd introduced them. Although he could still see that cautiousness that came with new riders, he also saw her reaching for something more with each tentative stroke she gave Tildy's neck.

He couldn't make out what she was saying to the horse, but whatever it was, Tildy seemed to enjoy it because she lowered her head, a silent incentive given to encourage Keely to keep stroking her.

The sight of this picture tugged at him, making him ache with the idea that Keely would be leaving soon, and he'd quite possibly never have the opportunity to experience this kind of simple yet profound joy again.

Another few strokes, and Keely stepped back as the horses took off. She fell in step with Jacob and they made their way inside the cabin.

"You want me to make you a snack? I'm sure I can find something to put together quickly."

He took her hand, squeezing it to give her the support she needed in this moment.

"I'd rather we sit down and talk. With so little time before you leave, I just want us to clear the air."

He stroked his thumb across a tiny patch of skin on the back of her hand, continuing their physical connection as he led her to the sofa.

Even after they sat, he kept her hand enclosed in his because things just worked better when they touched.

"I was afraid."

He took note of the honesty shining in her eyes, but remained quiet. This was her moment, and he needed to step back and let her have it.

"Things were fun, and even though there were a few moments where I questioned the wisdom of us hooking up, it felt right. It felt like we were headed in the right direction."

He agreed. Things felt right when they connected.

"But your little slip of the tongue at the dinner with Ezra sent you careening into a dark place that has made it easier for you to hide yourself from me than talk things out."

Her eyes widened with surprise. "I notice everything about you, Keely."

She seemed to take his admission in stride. But he knew from the way she sat stiff next to him that she somehow struggled with this idea.

"Jacob, this thing between us… It started with this explosion of friendship and sexiness that I thought would keep things light and fun. I… I…"

She shook her head, looking up to the ceiling as she searched for more words, he assumed. The only time he'd ever seen her so flummoxed was at the end of their dinner with Ezra.

"Keely, you deal with highfalutin celebrities on a regular basis. I'm assuming some of them are demanding as hell and you still manage to get through it. Why is talking to me so hard?"

"Because this matters," she softly replied before bringing her eyes back to his. "Because you matter in a way no one else has ever mattered before, and that scares me."

She turned to him, squeezing his hand as if it was an anchor she was checking to make sure it was still there, holding her steady.

She needn't have worried. Nothing and no one could've dragged him away from her at this moment.

Not when his heart was beating so fast in his chest he could hear its loud thumping in his ears.

"I have given everything to get where I am in my career, Jacob. My family still doesn't believe I have a real job. They're constantly questioning whether I can support myself, whether I'm thinking clearly enough about the future. And for the first time since I started Low-Kee Designs, I couldn't focus entirely on work."

She dropped her gaze from his and took in a long, slow breath before gradually releasing it through pursed lips.

"No, that's a lie," she continued as she lifted her gaze to his, revealing keen clarity. "It wasn't that I couldn't focus on work. It was that I didn't want to. I wanted to focus on what was happening between us. But before I realized it, I was allowing you to become more important than my career, making you my priority instead of my meetings, or the time I needed to increase my productivity."

Jacob could see the anguish slipping into the creased lines of Keely's brow. He extended his hand, running a gentle finger along her forehead, trying to smooth away those lines. He wanted to comfort her, but there was part of him that wanted to shake her too.

"I never asked to be more important than your work, Keely. As much as I want to fix things between us, I can't accept that blame. We had a deal. We wouldn't allow our connection to impact work."

She nodded, but even in her outward acceptance of his recounting of the preceding events, there was still something heavy and sad lingering in her eyes.

"We did make that agreement, and you're right,

you didn't ask anything of me. But I think that's part of why I was so preoccupied. I wanted you to ask that of me. And when I realized you hadn't, I started trying my level best to backtrack, to dive into work, but it didn't help. You were making billion-dollar horse deals and I could barely do a simple catch stitch."

"Well, now." His voice was tinged with a bit of amusement. "It wasn't exactly a billion." Her eyes turned into narrowed slits, further adding to his amusement and making him chuckle aloud. She was too damn cute, even when she was working through this quasi-existential crisis.

"I'm sorry," he continued. "I get what you mean. But the truth is, I was just as distracted. It was one of the reasons I wanted you at the dinner with Ezra. I knew I couldn't afford to be distracted by thoughts of you, so I figured if you were there, it would be less likely I'd drift off thinking about you when I was supposed to be entertaining Ezra."

She huffed, throwing her head back, and he could see some of the heaviness she was carrying press down harder on her.

He ached to make it better for her and for him. They both deserved it.

"Keely, it wasn't for lack of wanting that I didn't ask for more. Believe me when I say I wanted more. I was just afraid I'd push too hard and you'd run off. I made a promise that I wouldn't get in the way of your work. I didn't want to make you feel bad about doing a job you loved like women in my past did me."

A soft smile bloomed on her lips, instantly brightening the room while pushing away the dark cloud of worry that had marred her beautiful features.

"You want more with me?" She tightened her grip on his hand as she waited for an answer.

"Hell yeah, I do."

"But what about the distance between us? At best, it will take us four hours by plane to see each other. Are you really up for that?"

She wasn't wrong. Long-distance relationships weren't easy. Fortunately, Jacob wasn't known for doing things the easy way.

"I am."

Her eyes scanned his face, up and down, looking for any sign he wasn't being forthright. She wouldn't find any. He'd meant everything he'd said.

"Why?" She paused, looking into his eyes, her gaze cutting through flesh and bone until she was staring at the very core of him. "Why go through all this trouble for a woman you met three weeks ago who pretty much barged in and took over your house?"

He moved in closer, cupping her cheek and positioning his mouth so close to hers, all either of them had to do to connect was shift the slightest inch farther.

She licked her plump lips and he damn near gave in to the fire beginning to burn. But this was too important. He couldn't give in to the inferno that blazed so brightly between them, not when there was so much hanging on his next words.

"Because I love her…you, because I love you."

She was still. No, more like frozen. The soft intake of breath was the only sign that she'd heard him. His heart rate ticked up as he wondered if he'd gone too far too fast. But as the sound of his words trickled down around him, he realized he could never regret them. No matter how Keely reacted or whether or not she chose to have him, he needed her to know that he loved her, and probably always would.

"If you don't—"

The chance to complete his sentence never arrived because Keely had launched herself at him, taking them both down so that they lay across the cushions of the sofa. He had enough time to take in a quick breath before her lips were touching his, pressing urgently, marking her ownership of him.

And she owned him, of that he had no doubt. This glorious woman with her blunt words, her relentless determination and her amazing flair had swooped into his life, blowing away all the excuses he'd used to keep his heart protected. And he couldn't be happier about that.

"I love you too, Jacob." She shook her head, her shoulders shaking with brief laughter. "I've spent so much of my life designing every single detail of my work plan, that I hadn't considered I needed one for my life. You were an unexpected event, Jacob. One I will forever be grateful for."

"Good, because I feel the same."

He tightened his hold on her, loving the feel of her body on his. It was arousing as all hell, as was evidenced by his halfway-hard cock. But it was so much more than that.

Plain and simple, it was also comfort, making Jacob realize his mistake in his view of love prior to one Keely Tucker showing up uninvited into his life. He'd seen love as a hindrance, something that would detract from his dreams. There was no way he could've known that loving Keely would be the culmination of all his dreams coming true.

* * * * *

Look for the next books in the
Texas Cattleman's Club: The Wedding series

Four Weeks to Forever
by Karen Booth
and
Make Believe Match
by Joanne Rock

Both available March 2023!

Get 4 FREE REWARDS!
We'll send you 2 FREE Books plus 2 FREE Mystery Gifts.
DESIRE
BRENDA JACKSON
THE OUTLAW'S CLAIM
DESIRE
Married By Midnight
SHANNON McKENNA
FREE
Value Over
$20
PRESENTS
Unwrapping His New York Innocent
HEIDI RICE
PRESENTS
Forbidden to the Desert Prince
MAISEY YATES
Both the Harlequin® Desire and Harlequin Presents® series feature compelling novels filled with passion, sensuality and intriguing scandals.
YES! Please send me 2 FREE novels from the Harlequin Desire or Harlequin Presents series and my 2 FREE gifts (gifts are worth about $10 retail). After receiving them, if I don't wish to receive any more books, I can return the shipping statement marked "cancel." If I don't cancel, I will receive 6 brand-new Harlequin Presents Larger-Print books every month and be billed just $6.30 each in the U.S. or $6.49 each in Canada, a savings of at least 10% off the cover price, or 6 Harlequin Desire books every month and be billed just $5.05 each in the U.S. or $5.74 each in Canada, a savings of at least 12% off the cover price. It's quite a bargain! Shipping and handling is just 50¢ per book in the U.S. and $1.25 per book in Canada.* I understand that accepting the 2 free books and gifts places me under no obligation to buy anything. I can always return a shipment and cancel at any time by calling the number below. The free books and gifts are mine to keep no matter what I decide.
Choose one: ☐ Harlequin Desire (225/326 HDN GRJ7) ☐ Harlequin Presents Larger-Print (176/376 HDN GRJ7)
Name (please print)
Address
Apt. #
City
State/Province
Zip/Postal Code
Email: Please check this box ☐ if you would like to receive newsletters and promotional emails from Harlequin Enterprises ULC and its affiliates. You can unsubscribe anytime.
Mail to the Harlequin Reader Service:
IN U.S.A.: P.O. Box 1341, Buffalo, NY 14240-8531
IN CANADA: P.O. Box 603, Fort Erie, Ontario L2A 5X3
Want to try 2 free books from another series? Call 1-800-873-8635 or visit www.ReaderService.com.
*Terms and prices subject to change without notice. Prices do not include sales taxes, which will be charged (if applicable) based on your state or country of residence. Canadian residents will be charged applicable taxes. Offer not valid in Quebec. This offer is limited to one order per household. Books received may not be as shown. Not valid for current subscribers to the Harlequin Presents or Harlequin Desire series. All orders subject to approval. Credit or debit balances in a customer's account(s) may be offset by any other outstanding balance owed by or to the customer. Please allow 4 to 6 weeks for delivery. Offer available while quantities last.
Your Privacy—Your information is being collected by Harlequin Enterprises ULC, operating as Harlequin Reader Service. For a complete summary of the information we collect, how we use this information and to whom it is disclosed, please visit our privacy notice located at corporate.harlequin.com/privacy-notice. From time to time we may also exchange your personal information with reputable third parties. If you wish to opt out of this sharing of your personal information, please visit readerservice.com/consumerschoice or call 1-800-873-8635. Notice to California Residents—Under California law, you have specific rights to control and access your data. For more information on these rights and how to exercise them, visit corporate.harlequin.com/california-privacy.
HDHP22R3